1

Pulling on my workout gear and scraping my hair back, I strapped my band around my arm and slipped my mobile in the slot. My earphones were in place and my music blasting before I had closed my apartment door behind me.

My feet hit the path and I feel the freezing chill of a late autumn morning, my breath turning to vapour as I pick up the pace, chasing heat in the cold. It doesn't take long, my lean body finds the pace that toes the line, the balance of pushing myself further, faster but not too hard that I can't enjoy the rhythm and the challenge.

Running is my time. It is how I clear my head. The music helps keep my legs moving to the methodical rhythm I need, but I zone out the lyrics. Instead, I focus on the day ahead. Plan it through in my mind, what is coming, what needs to be done. Work. Work. Work. I can hear Amanda's voice in my head.

"*It is all you ever think about and I am SICK of it. This isn't a relationship. It is a fucked-up threesome, and not even the good kind where all three get off. It's like you and your work are having this... this love affair and I am just lucky enough to watch. Well, I am done watching, Frankie. I am done.*"

That was six months ago, a day later my apartment was emptied of any Amanda-related objects and she disappeared from my world as though she had never been part of it. Well, maybe she never really had been. Her point, whilst crudely made, was not inaccurate. I love my job, no—I fucking love my job. It consumes my thoughts, my mind, and I never switch off. It is what makes me so good at it. A thirty five year old female in a busy central city station and I am highly regarded in CID, the Criminal

LILY'S WORLD

A LESBIAN ROMANCE

MARGAUX FOX

Investigation Department, and whilst I am still a Detective Constable, I have my eye on Detective Sergeant.

My trainers pound against the concrete path, 5.30 am and the city is in transition—some returning home from long shifts or late nights whilst others are just waking to take on a new day. It is my favourite time of the day when I can feel two worlds colliding, the party girls meeting the early-morning vendors. The night owls making their way home as the early birds are rising from their warm beds.

I have had my share of both, early mornings and late nights. The job isn't a nine-to-five kind of deal, sure when I was desking it, I could fall into a routine but that is always short-lived. It may be a few days, weeks, even a couple of months, but soon enough I will become someone else. Dive into the murky world of criminals, lies and deceit, and I love it. The thill is exhilarating; the hunt and the chase make me thrive.

It was one of the things Amanda couldn't understand, that no one could understand really. That the things that others thought were bad about my job—the irregularity, the danger, the risk—those are the things that I find almost addictive, finding the thread and following it, weaving myself into their world until I belong, poised and ready to strike. The entire process, I live for it. Unfortunately, it doesn't make me great girlfriend material.

My body is starting to ache, my muscles stretched and used, I can feel the sweat now on my skin, the kiss of autumn is welcome against my heated body. I focus on my breathing so I can keep the pace without breaking my stride. My mind flicks through the day ahead, I am still desked but can feel the buzz in the air that an op is coming, whether it will involve me or not will depend on the area, the crime, the department, but the sudden lack of my boss being around is a good indicator that something is brewing. Our team's speciality is undercover operations across the region. There are five in our team and as two of them are already out in the field, I like my odds of being next.

My feet need no direction, I cover my usual route with little thought given to it and I arrive home in good time, not my best but not far from it either. I peel the Lycra from my skin and head straight for the shower. I read in some magazine years ago that hot and cold showers help your skin and speed up your metabolism. I have no idea if it's true but for years now I have showered in the heat with intermittent bursts of icy cold water. The shock factor makes my toes curl and my body scream at the unfairness, but it is refreshing; it makes me tingle.

I get ready with little thought given. I have never been a particularly girly girl, preferring comfort over style. I'm tall and physically fit. Running is my obsession and it hardens my body. My features are... striking. Bright green eyes often make people glance and then look again, my cheekbones are high and defined, which makes my face a little angular particularly with my thick dark hair up in my preferred ponytail. Once, as a teen, I had chopped my hair off to a short pixie cut that was all the rage... I had never made that mistake again. I don't do dresses unless it is needed to assume an undercover identity for work. I wear black jeans and fitted shirts as preference. I ditch skirts for sweats and I prefer the sports section to the heels and bags.

I don't hide the fact that I am gay. I mean, it isn't my opener, but I am always open with it. Sometimes guys take this as a challenge, which just makes me pity them for the time they are wasting. I'm not 'one of the lads' either. I take no joy in rating girls or engaging in that whole chauvinistic-style banter.

I'm pretty much insular with one friend at work, a great friend actually, Josh. He gets me, and after the first and only awkward indecent proposition he made me years ago, he has never so much as tried to dip his toe in that water again. In fact, since then he has married a stunning woman, Sarah, and had a baby. We keep our friendship a little under the radar because even though on Friday he was Josh with baby puke down his front sliding me a beer across his kitchen counter whilst Sarah ordered in pizza, at the station he is DS Cole; my boss.

He wasn't my boss when we met but he had been in the force a few years longer than me and well and truly deserved the promotion, there was no jealousy or envy on my part, and through years of working together, he has become my boss seamlessly. I, of course, respect the new line, he is my superior officer and therefore I certainly show him the respect he deserves, but he also knows how I thrive, what makes me a good DC, and gives me a little more freedom than I have had before, which has led to some great results for me, him and the department in general.

I am thinking of Friday night pizza as I stride into a coffee shop near my home. I have never been in this one before but I feel like Monday mornings at 6.30 am are made for something hot and sweet. So, I glance at the chalkboard and order a vanilla latte to go from a barista who can barely contain her yawns. I watch as she works the machine, she is on autopilot and it seems as though she could do it in her sleep, within seconds the smell of freshly ground beans and steamed vanilla milk fills the air, and I know I have made the right choice.

She hands it to me with a sleepy smile and in return, I tip her and turn to leave. I like to think that I am pretty aware of my surroundings and my peripherals are constantly in check, but this woman collides with me and it takes me a second to even process what is happening.

My reflexes kick in, holding the hot coffee away from either of us so the only casualty is the coffee and the floor, but she barrelled hard into me, catching my shoulder and almost spinning me off balance. She is slim, tiny in fact, and the impact sent her ricocheting backwards and spilling the contents of her purse, which seems to be a bunch of change strewn across the floor.

"Shit!" she exclaims with a southern drawl not native to the city. Most people would drop to the floor, apologetic, scrambling for the change, but she looks straight at me with no sign of any hurry, her lips curling into a grin. "Guess this could be awkward."

I am thirty five years old. I have felt the pull of attraction before, I can appreciate a beautiful woman, even feel the tingle between my legs at a suggestive glance. But this woman... is totally different. She is obviously younger than me, but I have a feeling she looks a lot younger than she really is. It seems as though she has not slept, her tangle of blondish brown hair is in a long unruly bob and she has a soft smear of black under her eyelashes from yesterday's makeup, but her blue eyes shine with an alert clarity. Her features are soft, feminine, and she is most definitely not dressed for the weather. Bare legs slipped inside cute ankle boots that glint with a silver star on the heel and a thick cardigan is pulled around her slim frame. I can't even tell if she is wearing a skirt or a dress underneath it, there is no hint that she is, in fact, wearing anything at all under the cardigan, but the flush in her cheeks and the way she keeps clenching her hands suggests she is freezing and is in need of some warmth.

The barista has already made her way to us with a mop and is cleaning up my discarded coffee. "I guess I should buy you a refill," she says with a slight raise of her eyebrows. I glance down and see that there is still more than half left.

"It's fine. I have to go anyway."

She nods but does not attempt to move

out of my way, so I have to edge around her. She still hasn't bent to pick up her change and so much of me wants to stay... to talk to her, to see that smile, to know her. But I feel like I already do know her; a woman who wanders into a coffee shop so early in the morning after being up all night, without a hint of an apology in her expression; eyes I could drown in and lips I long to kiss. Oh, I know who she is all right. She is going to be a big heap of trouble and that is exactly what my life doesn't need right now.

I give myself a mental shake as I leave and continue down the pavement to work, the streets are starting to fill and I weave my way in and out of the crowds. I take a sip of my latte, it is hot, creamy and sweet, just like her, and it is with that thought I toss the rest of it in the bin and push her firmly out of my mind.

"DC MILLER, do you have two minutes?" DS Cole shouted to me through his open office door. I look up from the pile of paperwork I am working through but decide it is best not to debate. "Sure thing," I call back and lock my PC, making my way into his office. Before I can take a seat he nods to the open door and says, "Close the door."

I raise my eyebrows but do as he asks. DS Cole is generally an open-office kind of boss so closing the door means one of two things: it is personal or something he needs my confidentiality for work-wise, and the tingle that rushes through my body tells me it is work-related.

I take the seat opposite him. "How can I help?"

He pulls out a report file from his top drawer and opens it. I can see photos and clippings from the recent robberies across the midlands that have been causing traction in the news. It is more of a specialist unit case so whilst I have kept my eye on in it, I haven't really been following it too closely. But now seeing the folder my interest is certainly piqued. "Have you been watching these? In the news, I mean?" he pushes the file across to me.

I pull a face of regret. "Honestly, not much if I am being totally truthful. I mean, everyone has been talking about it, what is it... five, six banks now, but I didn't think it would land on our desks so I kinda didn't give it too much thought. I figured special crimes would be all over it."

"Well, you're right, Frankie, they are all over it and getting precisely nowhere, which is why we have been..." he pauses finding the politically correct word "...*encouraged* to have a look. Maybe we might see something they're missing. Anyway, it has all been happening right across the region so sure, I have taken a look and been through the details, but I didn't catch anything that they might have missed. You said five or six, right? Well, it was six... until last night. Last night made seven. Which I don't think has hit the headlines yet, but I am guessing it won't be long before it is all over everywhere. Only last night was different."

I lean forwards. "How so?"

Josh looks up to make sure the door is completely closed before he turns his computer screen round to me. On it is CCTV footage of which I can only assume is from last night. I move closer and recognise Church Street straight away, it is one of the main high streets that run through our district in the city centre. He presses play and I watch the scene unfold in grainy black and white. It is the same as the others I have seen on the news. A van pulls up and cuts off most of the view, but two figures in black exit from the back, one from the side and the driver remains in the van. I see the bank door open automatically as though they have a key, except I know they don't. One of them, the smaller one, is holding an electronic device and whatever they're doing is hacking the bank's internal security system.

It is all over in less than ten minutes and I don't see much more than I already knew before. They set off no alarms, no one is in the building, the van out front deters any late-night walkers from even glancing at the bank, not that they would notice anything array anyway. They move with sophistication, seeming to know exactly what they're doing, and whilst there are four of them, they act as one. I watch until the van pulls away and then I look up at Josh.

"I guess they didn't leave much behind in terms of evidence?" I ask, and Josh grimaces. "Well forensics haven't finished yet, but let's just say it's looking highly unlikely that they left us a thumbprint."

"And what about the cyber team?" I sit even further forwards so I am barely balanced on the edge of my chair, taking Josh's keyboard I start to manipulate the CCTV, zooming in on the smallest figure and the device in their hand. They are wearing black from head to toe, gloves and their face totally covered. I can make out their frame, small, slim and petite. "Female," I say but it isn't a question. At this sized frame it is easy to guess that *they* are most likely a she. Josh just nods as I continue, "But the device, what is she using? Surely this is the key? How they are getting in and out. What do we know about her and that device?"

Josh pulls the screen back around to himself. "Well, that is just it, they don't know anything at all. In fact, it has the Detective Chief Superintendent in a complete fury, you know he isn't the biggest fan of the budget those guys take up in the first place, never mind the—"

"Stop!"

I cut him off and he pauses mid-sentence, but it isn't his words that have caught my attention. Everyone knows how the DCS feels about any department that eats into the budget and doesn't get results. What makes me stop him is a glint as he turns his screen.

I take it back and I take over the keyboard once more, angling and zooming. If he hadn't been turning it at that angle at that precise moment there would have been no way I would have seen it, but now I had, there was no mistake. As the pixels cleared and the frame became clear, the petite figure was paused exiting the back of the van. Her black jeans rolled up just an inch as she lowered her leg and there on her boot, just at the heel, glinted a small silver star. I move the video through on slow mo and the lithe movements of her body feel entirely familiar.

"Boss, I think I might know something..."

As a police officer, I don't believe in fate and I am not a huge fan of coincidences either, but it seems as though my coffee collision fits into the latter or maybe the former if you are a believer of that kind of thing. My friend Josh could see that look in my eye and know that I am onto something, however as DS Cole it is going to take more than that to authorise an undercover operation.

"Look, Frankie, I know you and I know that you're probably right, but no way can I start on this path without a bit more than a vanilla latte spillage with a girl wearing boots with a star on. You are going to have to go back and get me something, anything that I can work with to make this a credible lead. You get me that and I will get you undercover quicker than you can say Starbucks." I roll my eyes, but I know he is right and I would have say the same were I in his position.

So, I do exactly that, the news explodes with the most recent robbery and as it has moved into the heart of our city everyone is talking about it, everywhere I go. I, too, am now switched on and alert, picking up any information I can find. But the truth is, there just isn't much to go on.

I go back to the coffee shop every single morning. The day after I ask the barista about my collision girl under the guise of concern—was she okay, sorry I had to leave so quickly I was late for work, etc—but she doesn't seem overly interested in details and only said she seemed fine. I ask if she had seen her before and whilst she didn't seem overly convincing, she didn't think she had.

If it were me, I would have been certain, how does someone see a girl like that and forget her? But my hunt for her now is certainly job focused. I just knew those stars on the boots were the same ones in the CCTV, but if I am being honest with myself, those big baby blue eyes also have me drawn too. I watched the video of her at least a hundred times. I think I could pick out her walk in a crowd of a hundred, and whilst dressed in all black it was easy to see her petite, feminine figure, it was definitely her eyes in person that had captured my attention.

Now all I have to do is find her again.

I had run through a few options and tried to make sense of the pattern in which the robbery gang worked. It seemed to me that there wasn't much of one. Different banks each time, different areas; there was no correlation between security systems used. The amounts taken varied; the time of the robberies were all in the night but ranged from 1 am to 5 am. So, it was nearly impossible for me to see any kind of pattern.

But the last robbery had taken place at 2 am and I had collided with her at 6.30 am on the same morning. Which led me to believe that she lived or was staying in the local area, otherwise why would she still be here, or around here, hours after she had driven away into the night. It seemed strange that she would come back to the crime locality hang around alone at 6.30am.

It was that that kept me returning at 6.30 am for a vanilla latte, but after a week of being the only person inside the coffee shop when it opened, I had to rethink.

Heading round to Josh and Sarah's on

Friday with a six-pack in my hand, Latte Collision Girl is the hot topic of the night. Unable to discuss my theory much in the station I have waited until we are free from prying eyes so I can get Josh's take, and I can tell he is a little disappointed at my lack of progress.

"I have to be honest, Frankie, when I saw that look in your eye, I thought you might be onto something but even if it was her, realistically she just isn't likely to go back, is she?"

"Well not at 6.30 am she isn't," mutters Sarah, and I pause my sip of Bud. "What makes you say that?"

I watch Sarah fluster a little. She doesn't normally say much when Josh and I are talking shop, and I get the feeling that her opinion is sometimes not favourable in the Cole household when it comes to his work-life balance, but her statement has me curious. She clears her throat, "Let us just say you are right. Latte Collision Girl and Bank Robber Girl are one and the same and you did see her on her way back home after robbing a bank. You keep going back at 6.30 am except she isn't robbing a bank every night so why on earth would she be in there at that time? If she does go back into that coffee shop it is going to be for two reasons: one, because she has just woken up at a normal human time and wants a coffee... in which case you need to be in there at a more normal time. Or two, you need to make sure you are in there super early the next time she robs a bank."

I glance at Josh and he looks at his wife with an impressed raise of his eyebrow. She rolls her eyes. "I do listen, you know, and you would have got there eventually. I just really wanted to get there sooner so we can start talking about something other than Latte Collision Girl and the bloody stars on her boots."

I laugh and take another drink of my beer; I am relaxed but my mind is whirring ahead. Sarah is absolutely right, and Josh knows it too. We don't mention the robbery again and instead have a night of Cards Against Humanity, more beers and lot of laughs, but as he sees me out the door he says,

"Have your phone on. Next time they strike, you'll be the first person I call, okay?

But maybe start getting decaf or you might end up with a problem."

I forgive the Dad joke because that tingle of excitement makes me feel like we are on to something.

2

I live in the centre of the city but I spend a big chunk of my salary on an overpriced one-bed, one-box-room apartment. Not because I care for the fancy entrance, the elusive postcode, futuristic kitchen or my power jet shower, although I don't complain about that either, I just love the fact that I can be in the very centre yet sit out on my teeny tiny balcony and feel so high up out of the hustle and bustle. The view is stunning, and as I barely have a social life and I couldn't tell you a Prada from a Primark, it is my one splurge and my haven.

Not many people get an invitation either, I think even Josh and Sarah have only been a handful of times. I like my space, my me time, and this is where I come to escape the outside world. As my family lives way out of the city, they never have much need to drop by, and it is always me heading out to see them usually with a list of things my Mum wants from the high street shops.

I don't stop my routine with the coffee shop, even over the weekend though it passes by uneventfully. I don't think that I will see her, Sarah is right, but I think it would be suspicious to now break the routine. The waitress doesn't even ask me what I want anymore and I am pretty sure she starts heating my milk now before I walk through the door, but I do start to take a seat. I want to be able to have a reason to hang around and it not seem suspicious so I take a book with me and park myself in there for an hour on Sunday morning. I actually quite enjoy it. I can't remember the last time I read a book, though I am not sure how much of it I actually absorb. But the feeling of relaxing is nice.

I get to work on Monday and face the mountain of paperwork that just never seems to end. For every amazing day I have on the job undercover equals a million pieces of paper I have to work my way through when I return; and for half of it I am just repeating the same thing in a different way. It's the side of the job we all hate, but it is necessary when it gets to court time. These pieces of paper can make all the difference, and I have seen way too many criminals set free because one sheet of paper was misfiled, lost or just never completed. I slug my way through and make it through another Monday in the station. I try not to let it show but it is starting to pull me down a little, I'm getting the itchy feet to be back in the mix.

I pick up takeout on the way home, I can't be bothered to cook and I get an early night.

My alarm goes off at the normal time and I pull myself out of bed ready for my run, except its 3 am and it isn't my alarm, it is Josh. He cuts the call before I even answer, but I don't need him to tell me. Adrenaline surges through my veins because I know. I know I am going to see her. She is going to leave the robbery, head to the point at which they stash or share the cash, lay low and then make her way home past our café. Maybe she won't come in, but she will walk by—she has to.

I don't want to get there too early, it doesn't even open until 5 am anyway, so I take my run to use up some of the pent-up energy I have surging. I need to be calm and collected, cool and focused. I run so fast I make my fastest time, and I decide to take the stairs rather than the lift to really get my calves and thighs burning.

I take my time in the shower, think through the scenarios in my head, how I will act, what I will say. The goal will only be to get a contact number. I don't want to push, I don't want to scare her away, just a way to contact her... Facebook, Instagram, whatever she wants that will open that line of communication.

I pull on a similar outfit to the last time I met her. Only this time I hover in the mirror, thinking of those gorgeous blue eyes. I pull out an old mascara from my drawer. I hate to think how long it has been there as I run it through my lashes. I debate... hair up... hair down. I go for up; I think it suits me better... and then I give myself a mental slap. *Work, Frankie. It is work.* And I head out of the door.

THANKFUL that I have my book as a ruse, I sit and watch time roll by. My glance never once focusing on the words but on the street outside, looking for a glimpse of that messy golden brown tangle of hair, but not a peep. I get through two lattes and I think ordinarily I would be pushing my luck after nearly two hours at the table, but the barista seems unaware of my existence and every chance she gets in between customers she is on her mobile.

As I see the time inch closer to seven, I feel the buzz wear off. It really probably was just a coincidence, she could be anyone, going anywhere and I just happened to catch her along her route. I start to pack my book away as the door opens and the cold air sweeps through the café. I glance up and there she is, only she isn't looking at the coffee board, or the barista, she makes no move forward to order a drink. Instead, she is staring straight at me.

She is in a similar outfit, bare legs, boots, but this time a warmer jacket is pulled around her small frame. She runs her teeth along her lower lip in a slow seductive manner and they curl into a smile.

"I hoped I'd see you; I still owe you half a latte." She smirks and steps to the barista, I hear her clear as day, "A tea and half a cup of what she is drinking." The barista looks at her with a raised eyebrow but does as requested, and Latte Collision Girl glances over her shoulder at me with a wink. I watch her pay, cash, so we won't be able to get card details for her. Yes, I am still thinking about work. Although my eyes, starting at that silver star on her heel, have raised up her naked legs and glanced over the soft curve of her ass as she reaches to take the cups, and she looks back again at just the right second to catch my gaze, which makes me blush.

She makes her way over to me with a slow meander. I can see the goosebumps on her pale legs, she must be freezing. As she reaches my table, she hands me my half cup of vanilla latte and I take it from her. Our fingers touch, just for a second, and I feel that jolt of electricity. Her fingers are slim and delicate with chipped purple nails. I find the chips endearing, that she wears it because she likes the colour but doesn't feel the need to be perfect, plastic, fake. Then I realise my hand has lingered too long and I take my cup quickly.

"Are you going to ask me to sit or should I just stand around like a lemon?"

I raise my eyebrows at her confidence, most women are intimidated by me. I think my athleticism, tall frame and resting bitch face tend to give the back away vibe but she seems not the slightest bit perturbed, and without even waiting for me to answer she pulls the chair out with a loud screech across the floor and plants herself in it with a surprisingly heavy thunk. She pours a lump of sugar in her tea and stirs it with the slim wooden stick before sitting back in the scoop seat.

"You're my age, right? Do you remember when people used to smoke in places like this? Gross now, the thought of it. That dense, thick smoke lingering, sticking to your clothes and your hair and filling your lungs, but, you know, sometimes, I would just love a fucking smoke with my tea. Do you?" she asks as she holds the stirrer between her two fingers like she would a cigarette. I don't say a word but I give my head a soft shake. "Me neither. Not anymore, quit years ago, but I still want one, you know. You ever had that thing in your life that you know is bad for you? And you cut it out? But it is just a constant battle to not think about it? You felt that?"

She says all this so fast it takes me a second to catch up; she is a whirlwind. The conversation runs at a speed that makes me want to say slow down, let me savour you, I want to enjoy every soft word you speak. She leans forwards and takes a gulp of her hot tea. I see the little wince as she burns her tongue and then the satisfying shiver as the heat hits her, and then she looks up at me again expectantly. I clear my throat. "No, I don't think I have. I tend to do a good job of staying away from things that are bad for me."

"Sounds kinda... vanilla." She smiles to herself as she glances at my half cup of latte and the sweet scent of vanilla overwhelms me. I imagine that vanilla with her would be anything but, and I feel the flush spread across my chest as I think about those delicate fingers tracing over my skin.

"I think vanilla has a bad reputation, but if you give it a chance... vanilla can be so heavenly it makes your toes curl," I murmur softly as I take a drink of my coffee. It is actually too sweet. The barista has used the same amount of syrup in a half cup and it is almost sickly on my tongue, but I don't let that show as she watches me. I feel her eyes drinking me in, skimming the outline of my body, analysing my features. I wait, as though it is a test, and she doesn't respond for a few moments as though she is flicking through her options, weighing up the choices.

She stands slowly, tea in her right hand and her stirrer in the other still flicking it between her fingers like a reflex with no thought given to the action. "Seems like I need to try some vanilla. I will be here, tonight. Around 8. If you're around."

I watch her leave, and as her hand rests on the door handle, she turns back and faces me. I see her jacket gape at her chest and although it isn't possible, I am certain for a second she is naked beneath it, not a hint of clothing, just creamy bare pale skin. "I'm Lily, Vanilla Girl."

And with that she leaves, I have no chance to follow her. If I were more prepared, alert, in control of my thoughts and emotions I could have been out the door five paces behind her down the street, but the truth is... I am not. She has thrown me, just her presence makes my heart pound, and the thought of seeing her later fills me with a wave of lusty desire. I take the final sip of my drink, smiling as vanilla fills my senses, and make my way to the station.

3

"You have to know that I only got sign off on this because of how much shit the police are getting from the media. The DSU is giving you one week and the bare minimum in resources. You know the drill anyway but just let me make this super clear—get me something, *anything* that ties her to this and you'll have the full resources of the station behind you. But for now, you're pretty much on your own. And remember, if she is the brains behind this, you don't want her poking around your identity too much so share as little as possible. I know our tech guys are good with the stuff, but I thought banks were pretty good at keeping their doors locked too, so better not to chance it. You okay, Frankie?" Josh slows down for a second, and I give him the nod.

He is right; normally undercover would never be authorised and as it stands only myself, Josh and the DSU know about our mini operation, mainly because it is a huge shot in the dark and we cannot afford for any more fuck ups. I have gone undercover with minimal resources before, but the stakes were much lower then. I need to be on my A-game and I think Josh sees maybe a hint of misfocus and it concerns him.

"I am fine and I am ready," I say with a nod.

"Run it through with me again.

"Fran Edmonds. 34 years old. Birthday is 24th February. I work as a personal trainer. Single, distant with my family. Just moved into the city centre, looking for friends." I recite my back-up alias. We have a standard one ready to go at any point and after this op, Frankie Edmonds will fade away and I will be issued with a new one for situations like this. Josh nods and says, "You got this."

~

I LEAVE the station through the back exit; I am a little early for our 8pm meet and I highly doubt Lily would be in the area, but I just don't want to take any chances. I head back to the coffee shop and thankfully it is a different barista, otherwise I might be on a caffeine addiction list somewhere. I order a diet coke; I smile to myself as I see the coke with a vanilla option, but I stick with regular. I make my way over to the same table as this morning and I have barely sat down when there is a tap at the window beside me. I see Lily grinning at me through the glass, rolling her eyes as she spies my coke and beckons me outside.

I leave the drink unopened.

"Jeez, who takes a coke at like 8 pm. A diet one at that. I only said to meet at the coffee shop, surely you'd prefer a real drink?"

I glance down at my outfit, I haven't changed all day so I am still in my black jeans, a navy-blue t-shirt and thick black coat. Then I look across at Lily, she has her boots on but for the first time since I met her, her legs are actually covered... ish. She is wearing thick glossy tights and I see the hem of a patterned dress under her brown coat and the fur-collared hood is so adorably sexy on her. Her hair is still ruffled, but in this just ravished way and she has reapplied makeup in a style I could never do. It makes her blue eyes shine brighter than I would have thought possible.

"Helloooo... Vanilla... drink? Bar? Pub? Bit early for a club, but I am sure I could find us a place to let loose and get high..." She leaves that hanging and then nudges me with her shoulder, "Jeez, you are so... square haha. It is a joke. How about here?" She nods towards a pub that seems semi-busy; I have never been in before. "Sure," I nod and she steers us in from the cold.

She strides over to the bar and orders herself a gin and tonic. "I used to drink gin before it was pink and fashionable, I would just like to point out. What are you having? Diet coke?" Her lips slide into a smirk and I shrug my coat off with a roll of my eyes. "I'll take a Bud."

Her eyes scan my body, as she takes her

gin and my beer sliding cash over the bar top before leading us to a booth. The atmosphere is relaxed, and the leather booth seats are soft, which shows they've been sat on a lot but not cracked, so well taken care of. Lily shrugs herself out of her coat and I smile as I see her dress; it wouldn't look out of place in a music festival, the cotton is thin with bursts of coloured flowers. It hangs loosely from her body. She really is tiny, like a little doll; I am surprised the cold doesn't affect her more than it does. She sips her gin peering over her glass at me, so I decide to start the conversation.

"What did you do today?" I mentally shake my head. Was that the best I could come up with? I watch Lily grin at me and I feel like she can read my mind.

"Well... I slept. A lot. I was exhausted. Had a late night, that's why I didn't stick around with you this morning. When I am tired, I start talking about all sorts of crap. I wanted to make a good impression. Soooo, I went home, slept, woke up, did some boring stuff and then came to see if you would show up."

I pick up my Bud and take a slow sip,

the bottle is cold and the beer feel sensitive against my teeth. "You didn't think I would?"

She sits back in her seat and crosses her legs; I watch the hem of her dress inch up her thighs revealing more and more of her glossy tights. She looks contemplative, running through words in her mind trying to attribute the right ones to her thought.

"No, Vanilla. I wasn't sure. You are a bit hard to read. I think I can read people pretty well, you know; my Nanna was a bit of an empath and I think I have some of that in me. I tend to be able to figure a person out pretty quickly but from you... I got nada. Nothing. I can't even tell if this is a friendly drink or a date." She says the last word with a sly smile and hides behind her gin.

Work tells me this is a friendly drink.

The rest of me tells me it's a date.

"What do you want it to be?"

"See, right there..." She shakes her head "Well, Vanilla. I guess I would like it if it were a date; I love this tall strong shoulders thing you have going on and these intense eyes of yours that promise the green of an entire forest; if I look at you, the way you dress, the way your nails are short, something about your look, I assume you are into women. But, I should know better than to ever assume. I'm open to being friend-zoned as long as it is early on as my heart can't take a great fall."

My heart races and I feel my cheeks flush. As she takes another long drink of her gin, her loose dress slips a little on her shoulder. A few inches of pale creamy skin on show and the shine of her collarbone, and I long to kiss along it, to graze her skin with my teeth. I have never felt desire like it. It bubbles up inside of me and it is like I have no control. The words escape before I can stop myself.

"I would like it to be a date."

I feel her leg stretch and her calf runs up alongside mine, she leans forwards in her seat and I mirror her, matching each move she makes into my space with my own into hers. Her hair falls forwards, wisps of tawny dark blonde covering her left eye. It is an instinct; my right hand leaves the bottle of my beer and with cold fingers, I brush the curls away.

She jolts... I don't know if it is from the chemistry of my touch or the iciness of my fingertips against her skin. I pause... waiting to see how she will react, but she just turns her cheek so her soft warm skin brushes against my palm. It is a delicate touch, barely a glance, but as her eyes fix on mine, I feel a shiver myself that runs straight through my body.

"Let's get out of here," she murmurs, and I am standing before she has finished the last word.

WE BARELY SPEAK as we barrel through the streets. Lily is a force to be reckoned with—lithe, petite, she looks like a strong gust could blow her away and yet she moves with a vivacious ferocity. Her fingers knot with mine as she leads me, always one step ahead. Her coat not even fastened so it blows open in the cool October winds, but it is as though she burns hot constantly and never seems to notice.

We take a left down Grafton Street and she pulls me through the gate of one of the old Victorian terraces. She fumbles with her keys in an old, worn lock, and even when the lock clicks, she has to raise her knee with a thud to get the door to swing open.

The house has been converted into two flats; it isn't uncommon in the centre. Twice the rental for the same property. The downstairs left has another lock but she leads me up the narrow staircase, the dark blue carpet is worn, curled and faded from years of use and not much love.

This door opens easier and she leads me into the darkness, her fingers reaching down the wall for the light as she pulls her boots from her feet. I slip out of my trainers as the room lights up, and it isn't what I expect.

Apart from one room that I assume is the bathroom, the rest is just a big open space. A small kitchenette fills one corner, but the rest of the space is dominated by two things; a big double bed that is sat flush against a big bay window and then a huge desk, which is home to the most complicated-looking computer setup I have ever seen in my life.

Lily follows my gaze and gives a shy smile. "I am a secret nerd but don't worry, I hide it well. Um, would you like a drink? I don't have Bud or Coke but I have some wine, or I think there might be some vodka in the freezer."

I wander over to the computer. "Wine... Vodka... Whatever you're having." My fingers trail against the back of her leather desk chair and I push it so it spins to face me. I imagine her sitting here, planning her next robbery, mapping it all out in her leather throne, ready to take her next bag full of cash. I turn and sit and give myself a tiny spin until I am facing the five display screens in front of me. My hand reaches forward to the keyboard, I wonder if it is just on sleep; if the press of a button will bring it to life...

Before I even touch it, the screens come to life. They light up the entire room, and I sit back in the chair watching the synced displays showing an aquarium bursting with colour and life, seconds later the speakers begin to play. The music is low, a jazzy blues I am not familiar with but I like, and I look to see Lily approaching me with a bottle of wine in one hand and her tablet in another from which I can she is flicking through songs, controlling the displays from the palm of her hand.

"Let's set the mood, shall we..." She says with a smile, and instantly the blues fade into blacks and a starry night sky appears. It is incredible really. The display must be super HD; I feel as though I could touch Venus through the screen.

"Who knew nerdy could be so romantic," I whisper, and she laughs giving the chair a gentle spin so I turn slowly to face her.

She reaches past me, setting the tablet on the desk and the bottle on the floor beside us but she doesn't move back out of my personal space, instead, she invades it more. With a gentle shrug of her shoulders, her coat falls and then I feel those silky tights brush against my legs as she carefully rests on my lap.

Her knees slide wide, sitting high above me, straddling either side of my thighs, and I hear my own deep breaths as she lowers down slowly. My hands grip the arms of the chair tightly, almost afraid to move as her fingers run over the top of my head to my hair tie, which she pulls free slowly. I feel my hair fall, and in seconds her fingers are there running through my thick dark brown locks.

Her chipped nails trace lightly along my jawbone and she softly tilts my chin upwards; I feel her breath wash over my skin and I can almost taste the gin on her tongue before our lips even meet. The next touch is her hair, tracing over my face so my eyes flutter closed, then it is the tip of her nose, lightly brushing against mine in an Eskimo kiss that makes me smile.

But my smile is stolen by the graze of her teeth along my upper lip, which she then traps and pulls at lightly. It isn't a hard bite, but the contrast makes me gasp and my eyes snap open wide as her tongue dips into my mouth. I let go of the chair, one hand reaches up high and takes those curls that look darker in the dim light, with a needy grip, pulling her lips hard against mine. My other hand runs up the back of her thigh, gliding along her tights under her dress where I take a palmy handful of her fleshy ass cheek.

She gasps and my fingertips dig in, showing my want and need for her and she returns with a dirty dip of her tongue in my mouth that sweeps and swirls tasting all of me. I thrust my hips upwards, craving the press of her body against me, and she lets out a tiny soft moan as we press hard together.

The chair isn't working for me. I can't get enough of her like this and I need more. She is shorter than me and she is slim and light. Both of my hands drop to her ass and I rise with her in my arms. It only takes three steps and I find the edge of her bed where I drop her gently and watch her lie back.

I strip myself down to my bra and panties, they are black, cotton, sporty. They are nothing special and chosen for comfort. I feel her eyes run over me. I am confident with my body; my legs are muscular, my abs have the faintest lines of definition, which are how I like them. My ass is finely muscled and whilst my breasts are small, they are high and pert. My shoulders and arms are strong from the weights I like to lift in the comfort of my own living room.

Lily moves to strip herself but I stop her, catching her wrists and gently moving them away. I want the pleasure of unwrapping her. I take the bottom of her dress and pull it up slowly as I climb onto the bed, higher and higher revealing her inch by inch. Her panties are pink with watermelons on them, hidden slightly under her glossy tights, which are pulled right up to her navel.

I drop my head as I continue to undress her, and my lips trail up her body, over her stomach, the valley between her breasts, which strain against her pink bra, until her dress slips over her chin and I pull it through her hair. She shivers, but not from the cold. I search for her lips, giving them the softest of kisses before I work my way back down her body.

I reach her bra first and my hands slide around her back to flick the clasp; the instant it clicks the material loosens and falls away. She unravels her arms from the straps and finally, I get a glimpse of her breasts. They're bigger than I expected given her frame, both of my hands slide greedily up her ribs to take them in my palms, rolling her rosy pink nipples between my fingers and thumbs, she lets out the lightest of moans and it makes me nearly crazy for her.

My lips part and my tongue darts for a swirl around her hardening nipples, round and round until I feel her tremble with lust. I don't want either to get jealous so I alternate between left and right, and the one I leave unattended my fingers continue to tease so she feels the shocks of pleasure continuously rippling through her.

Her back arches and I can see the flush against her skin, so I leave her breasts in my hands as I continue my path downwards with my mouth. As I reach her tights, I take them in my teeth, ripping a little hole with my canines, which I then pull at so they tear apart. Crawling down further and further my hands have to let her beautiful breasts go, but they do so regretfully. My fingertips draw lines down her skin as she lifts up her ass so I can peel down her panties. I watch the fabric ride the curve of her delicious cheeks that I just want to sink my teeth into, and then watch as they inch over her mound, down her thighs offering me the first glimpse of her hot wet heat.

I nearly dive in right there and then, but I decide I want total unrestricted access so I continue until she is naked and I have slipped her panties from her toes. My palms slide inwards and upwards along her thighs, parting her wide for me, and I watch as her puffy lips part, offering me her wet, silky folds.

I wish I had the restraint in me to tease her, to make her wait and beg, but I don't. My head lowers and my tongue runs straight through her velvety sex collecting her taste on my tongue. Fuck, she tastes incredible. I feel the tingle straight between my thighs, my own sex wet and needy.

It is like she can hear my body and she reaches down, her finger slipping under my chin, tilting my head up so our eyes meet and she beckons me up with a single glance. Whilst I have held the control so far, I know my body is a slave to her. I can't describe what she does to me, the way her teeth run along her lower lip as she pants, the sparkle in her eyes, the needy grip of her fingers as she pulls me up to claim my kisses once more. All of it makes me spin with lust.

I reach down quickly to pull off my panties, my bra follows, tossed aside and forgotten in seconds. Both of us naked now, I lower myself on top of her and when we cling to each other it is the feel of skin on skin and even in a cold October night, my skin begins to glisten with sweat as we move together.

The press of her thigh against my clit makes me moan, and she too lets out a deep gasp as I mirror the action. Long slow thrusts of our bodies, leaving shimmering trails of our wetness on each other's skin. I'm on top of her and so much bigger than her. I wrap my hands in her hair, attacking her soft sweet lips with deep raw kisses, panting and gasping as we work each other's body higher and higher. I feel her start to shake, her muscles tensing and my hand drops to take her breast in my hand. With a hard squeeze of her thighs as she grinds against me, pleasure overcomes her and I feel her orgasm hard under me. As her juices cover my skin and I feel each wave of her crashing climax, it takes me over the edge. Her name is on my lips as I too orgasm and collapse onto her, and it seems to never end. Something that would have never previously resulted in orgasm for me has taken me there almost too easily. Over and over, I ride each wave until I am too sensitive and my body begins to jolt at the slightest touch against my pussy.

Untangling my legs from hers, only so I can take the edge off the burst of sensitivity, I roll off her and lie down beside her pulling her to me, wrapping her up in my arms. She looks up at me, her breaths still uneven and her lips swollen, she says with a cheeky smile. "I guess vanilla can be kinda fucking amazing."

I WAKE and am totally disorientated. Early morning light fills the room from the second the sun rises as the huge window dominates the front wall and the curtains are still open. Lily swears under her breath and reaches in a sleepy fumble to draw them closed before she lays back down again and within seconds, I hear her breathing change as she falls back into dreams. But for me, it is already past my wake-up time and I know I won't fall back to sleep.

I glance around her open-plan space and I know that snooping is impossible. I wouldn't even know where to start, but tech guys have to know what they're looking at. So, I reach over for my jeans and slide my phone out of my pocket taking a photo of the desk area. I hope they can take some details from it but even if not, at least I will have something to show Josh, albeit not much.

I don't look at my messages or anything else. I just lie back and close my eyes and try and clear my thoughts, normally I would go for a run to help with that, but I don't want to leave now. I have made that mistake before, where I have left at my normal wake-up time and it has been seen as a negative.

I can't believe that I had sex with her. Well, I can. I wanted it the moment she collided with me in the coffee shop, but my job is everything to me. Literally, my job is my world, and I could lose it all for this. I know if I went to Josh as a friend and asked him to cover my ass he would, but I already know in myself that I am not going to do it. That I have a unique chance lying here in her bed and I don't want to throw that away.

Plus, I really, really, *really* want to fuck her again.

And as if she reads that thought I feel her turn towards me, and her hands snake around my waist and begin a slow trail downwards between my thighs.

I don't think about running again all morning. I choose to lose myself in Lily's World.

4

The curtains are pulled open once more but only a little to let in a stream of daylight that softens the darkness in her open-plan room. With condensation running down the panes, toasty on the inside and chilly out, it is a reminder that we are locked away, a world of two. I watch her from tangled sheets, she is wearing a long nightie, maybe an old t-shirt repurposed. Because she is so tiny, I imagine that everything would look big on her. It looks like a man's shirt. But I don't let my mind wander too far down that path, not because I care in the sense of her being bi if she is, but I haven't actually asked anything about her current relationship status.

She opens the fridge and glances back at me; she looks adorably sexy, makeup smudges and her messy hair. "Eggs and toast?" It is my stomach that answers with a low growl and she giggles. She has a smile that lights up her face with its mischievousness.

I watch her as she moves around her kitchenette with ease, reaching instinctively for the things she needs. She hums a song under her breath. I can't place it but she moves her body to a rhythm only she can hear. Her shirt skims the cheeks of her ass, every time she reaches up, she gives me subtle peeks of the curve of her ass. It makes me a different kind of hungry…

I sit up and lean against the wall as she makes her way back to me with plates piled high with eggs and buttery toast. "For you, Lady Vanilla." She hands me one with a smirk as she climbs on the bed and sits crossed-legged with her own plate balanced.

"I don't know your name," she says with

a frown as she takes her first mouthful. I pick up my toast.

"I don't know yours," I say before taking a bite with a crunch.

"Yes, you do. My name is Lily," she says with an eye roll.

"Lily what?" I reply and she bursts into a grin.

"Oh, I see, you're going to stalk me. Don't bother with social media- I don't use it. My name is Lily Archer, I am twenty nine, even though most find that hard to believe, my birthday is on Christmas Day, which is awesome and sucks in equal measures. I was born in Kent, but I have lived all over. I have a brother, we're close." She pauses, a flinch, a flicker. I can't read it but she carries on. "I live here and I work in IT. Anything else you need to know before we... you know... oh wait... we already did that!" She gives me a playful nudge and continues, "So, Vanilla, what about you?"

"Me? I'm kinda boring. My name is Fran. I just recently moved to the city so I don't know many people. I am a personal trainer; I am a bit too focused on training sometimes. I nearly went for a run this morning when I woke, but I didn't want you to get the wrong idea so I worked out in other ways." I give her a sly smirk back, and I swear she blushes for a minute.

"Well, I for one am grateful for your training obsession. Your body is fucking beautiful." She fixes me with those intense blue eyes.

Now it is my turn to blush.

I continue to eat; the eggs are cooked just how I like them and I am hungry. With each mouthful, my stomach begins to fill, and I feel that rise of energy. My body feels the surge and my mind focuses. "So, what do you do in IT?"

I watch her fork hover against her plate, her mouth slowing as she chews as though buying herself time to think. She must be asked it enough, so I wonder why the pause, why she is hesitating to tell me her prepared lie. She takes an exaggerated swallow and then looks up at me.

"I guess you could say I am between jobs right now. Officially anyway. I used to work for a big corporation, but I left there a few months back, actually over a year now when I think about it. I don't think I am cut out to work for someone else. I freelance now, it suits me better. Being my own boss. But the jobs... well, they pay more but they're less frequent. A lot less earache too. Plus I don't have to be around people so much, and if I am being honest, I think a lot of people are idiots."

I can't help but laugh. I feel the same in general about people. Most of them annoy me and then the ones that you think understand you, that you think see things the same way, well, they just turn out to be a disappointment. Or worse. You disappoint them.

"And you? You like being a PT?" she asks inquisitively but with a genuine interest. It catches me off guard a little. Maybe because people are not usually interested in my real job.

"I like the exercise. I like working for myself. I like being able to choose my own lifestyle kind of thing. It maybe isn't forever, but I think I could do a lot, lot worse."

She nods. "I totally get that. My brother... he stuck himself in this job for years and he didn't even like it that much. He lost so many things for them, did whatever they asked. Gave his evenings, weekends, everything. Would have to go all over the country. His wife left him, barely saw her. I didn't even blame her, you know, he was married to that job more than her. They just took, took, took. Then ... they just decided to make some cuts. Didn't even tell him face to face. Just sent him a letter. Fuck. Makes me so angry, you know. That you can just become a number in the system. That you, as a person, don't mean shit." I see the anger burn in her eyes.

"Did he get another job?" I ask softly. She just shakes her head and I feel the conversation closing down. We have struck a nerve, and she has said more than she wanted to. "Well, I am sure he will. Someone like that, with a lot of commitment and dedication, someone will appreciate him for who he is." She gives me a smile, but it doesn't quite reach her eyes.

"I keep telling myself that."

WE HAVE A SLOW DAY. Just talking, chatting about random things. She is so easy to talk to that I have to constantly keep myself in check, but luckily when I ask her a question she answers with detail and depth. I listen to her thoughts and opinions, which are varied and filled with passion. Her eyes sparkle as she sits up straighter to tell me about her politics, she laughs as she recalls her younger wilder days and her eyes take on a serious glint when she speaks about her friends and family.

The lines are blurry in conversation. I keep telling myself I am working, I am getting more and more information, but the fact I am doing so whilst half-naked, or kissing her, or watching her with a burning desire means, really, they are not just blurry but pretty much none existent.

The day turns into evening and then fades into the night, but I barely notice the time. In fact, I lose all sense of it. Being in her presence is all-encompassing, and I start to lose sight of why I am even here. And the moments where I do remember fill me with dread, because the more time I spend with her, the more I fail to see how she could be committing the robberies. Not from an intelligence point of view; she is switched on, smart, educated, knowledgeable and I have no doubt she could do it. The thing I am finding more and more difficult to equate is *why*. She doesn't seem to care the slightest bit about money, and the robberies are committed not in some blood frenzy to show dominance but seem purely financially motivated.

Yet her apartment is modest, her clothes are high street, and her lifestyle seems no way focused on money or materialistic things. In fact, I would say the most expensive things she owns would be her technology— tablets, pcs, screens and things. Everything else seems like normal stuff everyday people would own, not a mastermind bank robber.

But I can't deny the truth. The woman in the CCTV and the woman who I am currently sharing wine with whilst playing Battleship are most definitely the same. I know her body intimately now but it isn't just that. It is her mannerisms, the way she walks, even how she holds her tablet and of course, those unique boots.

My phone lights up and I know it is Josh because only he can contact me. I look and he has replied to my photo, which of course I deleted. The message looks normal, between a client and their PT arranging a session for tomorrow. Of course, that run will involve him updating me and then I him. The thought already makes me feel conflicted.

"Are you okay?" Lily looks at me over the top of her wine glass. She circles it slowly before she takes a drink, but even as she swallows her eyes are on me.

"I'm fine, just a client wanting a session tomorrow. I don't mind but... I am happy here, you know." I say it and find myself realizing it is the absolute truth. Lily laughs.

"You know where to find me. Maybe you could stop off on your way back with some food. I can work whilst you're gone and then we can have dinner together? It is up to you, cook or takeout. I will leave it in your capable hands. What do you think?"

"I think..." I move my peg and make an explosion sound with my mouth as I take out another of her ships. I rest upon my knees, leaning forwards as I slip her wine glass from her hands. My lips part and I take a soft suck of her wine-stained lips before my tongue seeks a more thorough taste of her. I stay like that for a moment... minutes... hours... until when I pull back our lips are swollen and both our breaths are taken. "I think that sounds perfect."

It doesn't take long for the game to be left completely discarded and our bodies to become tangled once again.

5

I am meeting Josh for a 10 am run and I need to get to my place first to change, so I get up early and head home, hoping being out of Lily's apartment and back in my own space will give my thoughts some clarity. The truth is that I have to be honest with DS Cole about my investigation that is work, a professional relationship, and I won't hide anything from him that is needed for the case. The difficulty is hiding from Josh, who is my closest friend, my feelings for Lily and what we have been doing. Hiding it seems impossible; I feel like I have that freshly fucked glow and teenage giggles that he will see through in seconds.

As I head down to the city park, I feel the calm descend on me as my feet pound the pavement. Josh won't know about Lily and I being intimate because he will be in DS Cole mode. This job is too important, he will want the details and will be far less concerned with how I obtained them.

He is already there, stretching poorly, which makes me roll my eyes.

"Like this or you'll pull your hamstring." I come beside him and show him how to stretch properly and he does try and adjust his movements. After all, if this is going to be our way to check-in, he probably will pull a hamstring at that rate. "Ready?" I ask after a few minutes. He gives a grimace with a nod and I almost laugh. I know that running around the park would not be high on his things he would like to be doing right now.

Once we set off at a regular pace, for him anyway, he starts to talk.

"The photos you sent were useful. The tech team have managed to get some information that could be helpful for the case. Normally they would want you to hack into her system with a chip or whatever, but we have all agreed it is too early and puts you in too much danger. We have no idea what kind of security system she has in place, and whilst she might have this blue-eyed child-like look to her, she is still part of a criminal ring, and who is to say what they would do to you if your cover were blown." I nod and try not to think about those dazzling blue eyes. "The name she gave you isn't a fake. She really is Lily Archer. The registered address is correct, she has a passport, driving license and they're all the same person. So, she either really trusts you or has no idea how deep in this thing she is."

"Do you have any ideas as to motive?" I ask cautiously, hoping for an answer that would make Lily a little less guilty in the eyes of the law.

"Motive? Well, I mean it isn't a suspicious crime, is it? The motive would be to rob banks. Money of course. Why do you ask?" He looks across at me curiously.

"I guess she doesn't live a lifestyle that seems in keeping with bank robbing. Then the fact she hasn't given me a false name. I mean... I know I am pretty convincing undercover." I give him a cocky grin. "But I am new in her life and as a criminal, she should be wary, yet is open about her information. Just isn't all making sense to me yet." He thinks about it for a few moments, he tilts his head from left to right, visibly thinking through, weighing up.

"I don't think it will help much right now, but I will have a look through and try and find a motive. All the patterns are completely random... although I guess a motive might give us a clearer picture and then be able to find a clearer pattern. Yes, I will give it some time and see what I can find. I mean, they are profiling her. I haven't put a tag on her just yet. I know you're in the home, around and a presence. A tag would be helpful if we weren't already in but now I just think it would spook her. Okay. All you need to do is exactly what you have been doing. Playing a longer game is fine, don't push, but also try and see about her network, when is the next robbery going to be? Where? Those kinds of details are what's going to get them caught. I know you got this though, Frankie. Really. You are doing a great job."

I feel a stab of guilt. An ache in my side and I subconsciously move my hand, and Josh notices.

"You okay? Stitch?" he asks with a little concern; I just give a nod and slow my pace a little more, but the truth is far more serious.

I feel caught. I have already betrayed Lily's confidence in me and I have most certainly betrayed Josh's. I am walking a thin and dangerous line that could put many people in danger.

"Frankie, are you okay? You don't look so great."

I bend over and catch my breath a little, my head is spinning and it makes me take deep lungs full of air. I grip my knees and try and keep my focus, counting slowly in my head, finding my calm to ride the wave of panic and nausea. I don't get panic attacks often, not since I was a teen, really. I found exercise was a good way to deal with them, that and to have things clear and orderly in my own mind. I take a minute more and stand up straight.

"I'm fine, just pulled my side. Needed a minute." Josh reaches forwards to touch my arm with concern, but I back away from his touch. "Honestly, I am fine. Let's keep going."

We continue our jog around the park, Josh talks through a few more things but adds nothing new. I zone him out a little to try and focus and see if I can see a way out of the mess I am making, but no solutions come.

I DECIDE TO COOK. I think it is more thoughtful than a takeaway and a good excuse to get more comfortable in her space. I stop off at the store on the way to her house and pick up what I need plus a few extra treats. I am overthinking so I end up buying about five different meal options and about four different types of alcoholic beverages. I trudge to her apartment and I have to press the buzzer with my nose. I hear her laughing through the intercom as she buzzes me in and she is still giggling as she bounds down the stairs to meet me, grabbing a couple of bags from me to lighten the load.

As we tumble through the door, I catch her gaze, the laughter still lingering on her lips. She has changed, as have I. For me, it's a similar outfit to dark jeans that are tight to my figure and a low-cut scoop neck that shows the tops of my breasts as I slip my coat from my shoulders.

I think she will move closer, but she doesn't, she steps back into the center of her living room. My eyes are staring, my heart is pounding in my chest. We are standing a meter apart and yet neither of us move closer. I reach to the bottom of my top and pull it upwards, undressing myself slowly. My fingers fall to my jeans, first the button and then the zip. A slow undress as I peel the tight denim away from my skin until they fall to the floor.

I am wearing sporty black underwear again. Nothing else. Her eyes are drinking me in; the swell of my breast, my toned calves, the smoothness of my thighs, the outline of my collarbone, the curve of the waist, how my hair falls over my shoulders as I pull my hair tie loose.

She never looks away as her fingers work down the buttons of her dress, revealing her body inch by inch. I take in her frame, her shape, the subtle curve of her hips where her thin cotton thong rests. I step forward, just an inch.

I'm not wearing a bra. My breasts are not big, nor small, a handful, with small rose nipples, hard in arousal for her; she pulls off her bra and throws it to the floor then like a mirror she copies me and she too moves an inch closer.

I only have my panties left. I see her eyes on them. My legs are spread, just that thin black cotton blocking her from me.

Am I wet for her, does she wonder as she stares? She steps forward again.

She has nothing to be shy about, she is confident in her body and as her full breasts rise and fall perky on her chest, she slides out of her thong, leaving herself bare. She smiles to herself as she sees my body react to hers. My nipples harden, my chest flushes, my breathing becomes shallower, quicker. I hook my fingers in my panties and slowly I lower them, snaking my hips as I do, when I reach my knees, I let them drop and stand. My thighs parted slightly. The hair between my legs is trimmed neatly for her.

We have covered the distance between us. We are inches apart. I can touch her; she can touch me. My fingers move first. To her arms, her shoulders, over the swell of her chest, they are tracing her contours, memorizing every line, every curve.

Her hands move forward and take my nipples between her finger and thumb, they squeeze, hard. I gasp, the sensation sending shockwaves through my body directly to between my legs. She sees my pupils dilate, my lips part and she leans in and kisses me. Not a soft kiss; it is hungry, probing, tasting. My hands reach up to her soft hair, my fingers grip her curls in my hands as I kiss her back, nibbling her lip, hungrily tasting.

She squeezes my nipples again and a low moan leaves my lips. I can't control it and the sound makes her wetter, her hands drop to my ass and she cups it, pulling me to her. My wetness arouses her more as she pulls me against her thigh and then she moves almost instinctively to slap my ass, hard but playfully.

The feeling sends me over the edge, I break our kiss and lean back, my breasts exposed, and I move my hips so I can slide a little more against her. "Please..." I murmur.

With a push, she turns me and presses me face first against the wall. I feel her left hand on my hip pulling my ass slightly backward towards her before I feel the fingers of her other hand thrust into me, curling inside me towards my g spot with a hard, deep, push. She feels me stretch and open for her, two fingers held tight in the warm folds of my sex. With one hand holding my hip, she thrusts her fingers into me again and again. Harder, deeper, moaning with each roll of my hips.

I lean forwards into the wall, my hips angled back towards her. Riding each thrust to take her fingers deeper, and harder. I feel another finger push roughly inside me. My nails rake down the wall as I let the desire consume me, my orgasm rising within me, I feel it burning from the very core of my being.

She feels my spasms, she knows I am close, she is edging me closer and closer to the release I crave.

As my head rolls back my mouth opens for a long moan and my orgasm washes over me as my wetness gushes down the inside of my thighs. Well, that doesn't happen often. Everything feels different with her. She pulls her fingers out of me and instinctively brings them up to my mouth. I taste myself on her, her delicate skilled fingers pushing into my mouth and around my tongue. The scent of my sex is strong and my pussy aches once more for her touch. The action surprises me but I welcome it. I suck, my tongue circling the tip of her fingers, as she pushes in deeper. I suck harder, faster, teasing. She is watching me as I tilt my head back, hair falling down my back, taking her in my mouth. Her other hand slides up my inner thigh, collecting the wetness that has run down my skin before she slides into my pussy once more. She knows at that moment I am hers, that I would follow her wherever she led me. That her desires, wants and needs are completely entwined with mine.

"Fran..." she moans. My name on her lips is too much, I let go. Like Icarus, I have flown too close to the sun. I give in to the fire, the warmth, the burn and I orgasm... once... twice... who knows how many times my body comes for her? And I feel her too. My hand moves to her when I can, reaching inside of her. I feel the lust consume her, her body stiffening, her muscles tense and then a flood of wetness against my palm. I cry out with the intensity of my orgasm and the feeling of hers all over me.

We collapse on the floor. A pile of hot, sweaty bodies, entwined, still connected, wet from ourselves and each other. I glance out of the window; the night has fallen and the moon is the only witness to our moment of heaven.

WE AGREE on stir fry in the end. We are both starving and it takes the least amount of effort. I cook but it is a slow process. My legs are like jelly and I can't stop myself from looking at her, touching her, reaching for her at every chance I get. In fact, it gets so bad that I tell her she has to go and sit down or we will die hungry for food but our bodies aching from sex.

She pulls out a pop-up table and sets it all out, with wine, candles, the works. I dish up and serve steaming hot vegetable noodles dripping in hoisin sauce and crispy chicken. It smells delicious but as I sit down, I suddenly feel nervous and my tummy rolls with butterflies as I look up at her with a shy smile, she bites her lip and gives me a cheeky grin.

"Don't you go pulling those cute faces at me, I know you're not shy," she says as she curls her noodles around her fork and taking a big mouthful. I grin as she gets sauce all over her chin and reach forward to rub it away with my thumb.

"How was your day?" I ask quietly and she gives a slow shrug.

"Kinda meh. Like I didn't do much. My client is kind of trying to get me to take on more work, but I feel like I am over it now or at least I am not as enthused about the project as I was before. Anyway, they need me to tie up some loose ends, which I will do and then we will part ways."

"Oh? How long will that take?" I ask.

"Not long, I just need to map some things out then dedicate a night or two to it. Ideally, one but I have a feeling it might be two more. Then once that is done, I guess I will have to dip my toes in the freelance pool again and see what I can find."

"Is it competitive, your field? Will you find it easy to get another client?"

Her forks hovers. "Hmmm... yes and no. I mean the IT world is full of amazing talent, like any industry I guess, but I am really good. Well, actually I don't want to blow my own horn, but I am one of the very best at what I do so I know I will find something. The thing is whether I will like that something. What I am doing now... I started it with a purpose, you know. I had this... drive but my sails lost their wind..."

She lets that sentence teeter off and I am desperate to know what that drive was, and why it has now passed. What would make this incredible intelligent young woman turn to a life of crime and working with criminals? I can't piece it together.

I take a fork full of food too and my stomach sings with the first swallow, but at the same moment the buzzer to her apartment chimes. She doesn't look concerned but she makes no move.

"Erm, Lily, aren't you going to get that?"

"No," she replied unperturbed.

"But, it could be important? A friend or your brother or something. I won't say anything if you don't want people to know I am here, but you can answer it." I see a flash of something, not anger. Irritation, maybe. Frustration? It is hard to read.

"It isn't my brother, but fine. I will go and check." She stands slowly and she is definitely frustrated as she presses the intercom.

"Lilz, it's Spenn. Can you let me up, I need to talk to you about Thursday, the thing is we have a—"

"You can't come up Spenn. I am not alone. I have a 'friend' staying. Now fuck off. Message me if it is urgent."

She cuts him off mid-sentence and then kills the intercom. He doesn't buzz back up so he must have got the message loud and clear. I don't say anything as she sits back down, I wait for her to speak. The silence rolls on a little and then she gives me a little sigh.

"I'm sorry to have been abrupt, but I don't like people calling around unannounced."

"I understand. I'm the same really. I just thought maybe it could have been important. I am sorry. I shouldn't have pushed," I say apologetically.

"You didn't," she says curtly, but I know she is unhappy; she doesn't mask her emotions very well at all. The problem is that I am unsure if it is him or me that she is unhappy with.

"Is he your ex?" I ask cautiously and I watch her intently. Her eyes flick up with a confused eyebrow raised and then she laughs, a genuine laugh.

"Fuck, no," she laughs. " He wishes. I mean I'm really not into him. I am not gay; I'm more like... pansexual, you know. I have been with both guys and girls who have totally rocked my world. I am not really the relationship type exactly, but when it comes to connection and sex, I don't see myself choosing because of their gender. It is about the moment when you touch and the sparks fly, when you feel that closeness. I never asked you, are you gay or bi or... something else?"

"I'm gay. I can feel a connection with a guy, friends or something, but it is purely platonic. I have zero urge to be with him physically. I never have. I think I was about fourteen when I realized that I just didn't feel the same way as other girls did about the guys at school."

"You ever try it? You know? For curiosity?" I shake my head before she even finishes. "Really? I mean, I get it. If you know, you know, but most women end up fucking guys when they are young and figuring things out."

"There were moments I felt like I should, but I didn't. I am lucky with my family. We are not super close, but they have always been supportive. I mean, times were changing anyway when I was teen but still, it is not uncommon for parents to have an issue with it. Mine were surprised but accepted it really quickly so I felt no pressure there to be someone else. Do you tell people you like both? Did you tell your family?"

"My parents weren't exactly around much. They didn't care one way or the other. My brother knew. I told him... but not like, 'oh I like everyone' kind of thing. It was more just I dated a guy then I dated a girl so it was kind of obvious. He didn't care though, as you said, just wants me to be me and that's that. But no. I am not in a relationship with Spenn or anyone else for that matter," she finished firmly and I believe her, then she adds a little more hesitantly, "Are you?"

"No, I am single. My last relationship didn't end so well so I decided to give myself a break for a while. I wanted to get myself together and understand what it is that I want before I let someone else in again. If that makes any sense," I say with a wry smile but she just nods understandingly.

"It makes perfect sense to me." I look up at her and our gaze meets, and I swear for a second those blue eyes see straight into my soul.

"What about your friends? What do they think?"

She leans back in her chair and grins at me. "You know, I am a pretty open book. I don't hide who I am or how I feel. I'm a free spirit, but I am strong, independent and clear in my own mind how I feel. I don't need anyone's approval on how to live my life. So, my friends, the few I have, are real friends. Genuine friends who accept me just as I am. I don't need anything more than that. Obviously, most of them are down South. They are not from here and I don't see them as often as I like but we keep in contact. Anyway, what about you? I'm doing too much talking!"

I mirror her stance and sit back in my chair; I try to look relaxed but I don't feel it. She is an observer; she notices things and I suddenly realise I don't want to lie to her.

"What do you want to know?"

"Well, you haven't told me much about your friends or your family. I don't know what you like to do in your free time. I don't even know where you live." I see her settle in her chair, waiting patiently for me to tell her all about myself, but the words won't come easily about my family or friends so I focus on the real, the truths I can tell her.

"I live in the centre in the high rises. It is expensive but I like the quiet. I like that I am in the heart of the city, that it spreads out around me and I am in the beating hub of it and yet, I can open my balcony—that makes it sound way fancier than it is; it is tiny, just to say—but yes, I can step out onto there and it is just, quiet. I love that. I really love that feeling of being there and then not at the same time. It is my haven."

"It sounds magical. You will have to show me sometime. Although I might find it hard to leave to come back to here," she says with a smile.

"Oh, I don't know," I reply, looking around. "Here is... I wouldn't have expected it from the outside, but it is super modern and I love that it is an all-open plan. Makes it super spacious and light, that bay window is stunning."

"It's a funny thing, that window is the main reason I took this place. The last owner had these, like, Ikea partitions up so they could separate off the different spaces. They said I could keep them if I wanted them, but I figured the openness would be nice, the window being the focus of the room. It is a fucker for the cold though. It lets a draft through all winter and then heats up like a hotbox in summer."

"You have been living here a while then?"

"Nearly a year now. I came here after I left my corporate job. Needed to get out of my old place, you know."

"Why did you choose here?" I ask, and she takes a deep sigh.

"My brother. You ever heard of a person talk about a place and they just make it sound so amazing? He never lived here but travelled here a lot for work, and of all the places he went this was his favourite. I don't know why really, he just loved the city park, the people, walking along the river. *A city that seems like a town, Lilz.*" She ends with a change of her voice and it is obvious she is quoting him and I get that. For the population size and density, it certainly doesn't have that big-city vibe like other places do. Seems an odd reason though, just because someone else likes a place, to move her whole life here.

"Does he—" I start to ask just as she starts to say, "More wine?" I smile and raise my glass up so she can fill me up once more. "Oops," she says with a grin as the bottle only comes out in a dribble as we have finished the rest. "We had better try one of these other things you bought. Ooooh, gin!" she says excitedly as she pulls out the bottle, and before I know it, we are falling into bed in a tipsy haze.

6

"Do you think they're going to hit another bank tonight?"

Josh asks me in his DS Cole voice as we make our way around the city park. It has been raining all night so our feet splash in mud puddles, and whilst the rain has stopped now the air is still thick with drizzle, making it harder to breathe.

"No, well, it is totally possible, but logically I would have thought this would be more of a pre-meeting to plan or establish the next hit. You need her tailed, for sure, but unless they're all communicating in-depth remotely, I think they would need a pre-meet before they strike another bank.

Plus, they are all over the news. It is all anyone is talking about; the stakes are getting higher, and they know they need to be as flawless as before. That takes time, prep and planning. A new target, a new van, a new everything to make it clean."

"And you didn't see the guy?" I shake my head.

"No, like I said, I was inside, she just answered the intercom and she turned him away. You should check the CCTV for the area though; it was at 21.46 when he was at the door."

"Great, I will do that, although that was late for you to be there so great job for sticking around so long, Frankie."

His words are slightly weighted, but I don't react. I wonder if Josh knows the truth about what is going on on some level, but as a professional, he needs to not know about it.

I don't reply but my stomach twists.

"So, will you be seeing her tonight? Before she goes?" he asks, and I shake my head.

"No, we didn't make plans to see each other so I figured I would come into the station. I can be more use there." He looks over at me with a frown.

"Are you sure that's a good idea? I mean, we're running around a park now... You really think you can make it into the station undetected?" I look over at him with raised eyebrows. "Come on, boss, give me more credit than that."

I SLIP into the station through the back way. I know I wasn't followed but I still crossed over myself a few times to be certain. Just being back in this environment makes me feel better. Clearer. The lines are less blurred. No matter my feelings for Lily, she is a criminal, and if she does it again, she will be caught. I no longer have the burning urge, like in the beginning, to be the one to catch her. In fact, I would like to be as far away from that part of the operation as possible, but I know in my heart she should face justice.

The operations room is small, Josh had told me that there were only a few on them working on the case as they didn't want any leaks or any fuck ups. The Detective Superintendent is just leaving as I arrive.

"Great work so far, DC Miller. I am very impressed with how quickly you have brought us a workable lead."

"Thank you, Sir," I reply, and he gives me a curt nod before he ducks out of Ops Room 4.

The screens are all set up and the CCTV is running. There isn't a camera directly in front of Lily's apartment, but we have a view up the street from a nearby traffic cam that gives us a clear image of someone arriving or leaving. After that it becomes path mapping, hopping from view to view to keep them on the screen whilst our tail keeps behind her. They will have GPS tracking activated, which will assist with the CCTV mapping but isn't always reliable. After the fact, we can trace a lead pretty well but being live is open to many different factors, and it's a fifty-fifty chance as to whether we will keep up with her movements through the city. If she hops into a car it is easier with ANPR, Automatic number-plate recognition, the computer can do most of the work, but in the city centre on foot it is up to us to keep on her trail. With so many different possibilities it doesn't always work the way we hope so my expectations are always set accordingly. Still, there is a soft hum of excitement as we watch an operation come to life.

I take the seat beside Josh. I don't want to interrupt so I sit quietly observing. We have no idea when the meeting will take place, but if I had to make a bet, I would say about the same time that Spenn turned up at Lily's the other night, and sure enough around nine-thirty, I see her slim figure exit her building and make her way towards the camera as she heads outwards of the city centre.

I watch her, moving as though unobserved, not knowing all eyes are on her. She is not wearing enough clothes as usual, and even though I can't see in the grainy image I know that goosebumps will be lining her skin as the winds batter against her small frame. Not that it has ever bothered her as far as I can tell.

She slips her headphones in; I see the pace of her step change to fall into the same rhythm of the song. She knows exactly where she is going, no pause or hesitance in her course. She moves with a grace that entrances me, her walk is so smooth it is like a dance and I can't take my eyes off her. Then I think to myself, *Please, Lily. Just turn around and go home.*

But of course, she doesn't. Instead, she ducks into a shop. There is movement around me, Josh talking into the headset to whoever is tracking Lily, the CCTV operative changing angles, trying to find a name, there isn't one. Not one that we can see anyway. Searching, data inputted until a still street view appears on the screen: Spencer's Betting Shop.

"Well, Frankie, I think we found Spenn and where this money is being moved through. Now it is time to find the trail. You need to go back undercover and do exactly what you have been doing. We will chase down this lead, okay? Great job, everyone!"

I am smiling on the outside, but I feel like black clouds swirl beneath.

~

I GO BACK to my apartment, letting myself in. I don't even turn the lights on. I just sit in the dark and let my mind race. What am I going to do? What can I even do? The shop will be monitored even more than Lily now. Profiles will be made on everyone who comes and goes, the unit will get access to their financials, they may even get a phone tap, the net is closing tight around them, and it is because of me. Usually, this would fill me with pride. I would be buzzing, celebrating, feeling us inching closer to an arrest. But now I feel sick. The net is closing and Lily is in the very center with nowhere to hide.

In my dark living room my phone flashes and lights up the room, her message displayed on the front screen.

I know it is late but do you want to come round? L x

I do. Every fiber of my being wants to see her and be near her. I wanted to get lost in her soft skin, to kiss her until my jaw aches, to feel her body writhe so hard against mine that it feels like we have become one. But my mind can't take it, I can't bring myself to be around her and fall deeper in these feelings of desire knowing what is to come.

I can't tonight. Sorry. It sounds cold, my finger hovers before I add an *x* to soften the tone. Her reply is almost instant, but I don't enter the message just pull down the notification so she doesn't know I have seen. I climb into bed with the question etched in my mind. *Tomorrow? L x*

I STAY at home all day Friday. I don't want to be around people. I force myself to do all the tasks I hate to do, like scrubbing the bathroom tiles, cleaning the rubber in the washing machine and ironing all my summer clothes to box them away for winter. I just want to keep my mind blank, but it is there hovering and I know I can't ignore Lily forever.

Leaving her on unread seems cruel so as I finish the last mind-numbing task on my list, I pull off my rubber glove and slide her message open.

So sorry. Crazy day. Would you like to do something later? I don't even put my phone back down before she replies and the moment it flashes, I know the day of silence has done me no good as my heart leaps.

Perfect. Shall we venture out into the world or a cozy night in? L x

I know exactly what will happen if we opt for a cozy night in so I message back telling her we should go out. I don't make a suggestion but we agree to meet at our coffee shop at eight. I run through available options in my mind.

The trouble is that the best things would be where we can have minimal contact such as the cinema, but the issue with that is that we also can't talk in the cinema and right now that is what I need to do. I need to understand Lily so I can find us all a way out of this mess. I cannot tell her who I am. I can't stop her from doing what she is planning to do, but maybe I can guide her, make her see she has other options... Or maybe she doesn't, maybe she is being forced to do this? I don't get the impression at all that she is under any pressure, but I can't make it add up in my mind. It is like there is a piece of the puzzle missing and without it, the entire thing just doesn't make any sense.

I get to the café half an hour early and take a vanilla latte at my favorite table. It feels like forever since I have even been in here, when in reality it has only been a couple of days. I feel the gush of cold as the door opens and I glance up to see her. She grins at me. "Great minds," she mouths as she heads over to the counter to make her order.

I watch her, never in enough clothes but with a bounce in her step as she orders her tea and snakes herself through the tables to me. She settles in her seat and gives me the biggest smile.

"So... am I late? Are you too early? Are we both just bad with time?" She laughs and I smile.

"I thought I should get my latte intake before we head out. Have you had a think about what you want to do tonight? Any particular way you would like to spend your Friday night with me?"

"I had an idea, you can say no, but how would you feel about a walk along the river? We can get something hot to walk with, go down the river path? What do you think?"

"I think it sounds perfect." And really, I mean it.

We gather our drinks and make our way to take a slow meander down the river path.

"Did you know they redid this whole area a few years ago? That it used to be really bad along here for crime and drugs so the city invested a lot of money making the pathway. Cutting back all the hedges and trees so there were no dark spots and putting in all these cute street lamps so people felt safe, and then a café opened, a few more, restaurants, and now it is one of the nicest places in the city. Isn't it strange how that can happen? Just opening things up and letting in more light can chase the darkness away."

I do know that. Of course, I do. I used to work this stretch as a police officer when I first joined the force, and I would never have believed then, that I would be walking down here now like this. The whole left side of the banking was filled with crime. Mostly drug-related. Every morning the council would have to send a specialist cleanup crew just to remove all the needles. But she is right, the area has undergone a huge transformation. The apartments along the riverbank are now sought after, it is the hip area of the city where people want to be.

She slips her fingers between mine, and I am surprised by how warm they are. She runs on a constant high temperature. I feel my own hand warm in hers, feeling returning to the tips of my fingers.

"You were quiet last night and today. I tried to run through it in my head. If you were genuinely busy or if you were avoiding me. I decided that you were avoiding me. It isn't an issue; we have spent what seems like every second together since the moment we met. But. I have a feeling there is something more to it. You talk to me like I am a code that you need to break. You ask questions and I have never known anyone listen so intently. You seek truth and I feel compelled to tell things to you."

She is speaking softly, there is no anger

in her voice. Just a matter of fact. I don't answer, I just listen.

"I think that part of you knows I am hiding something. That there is a before and after in my life. A catalyst of change. Well, you are right, there is. A moment that came from nowhere and set me on a different course. I have never lied to you, Fran. I have never hidden who I am, but there is something you don't know. I told you about my brother, Kurt." As she says his name her hand tightens around me; it is a reflex, a reaction.

"We didn't have a great family life. My parents didn't give a fuck about us. My dad left us when we were young and Kurt was the man of the house. Mum, well she cared more for a drink than anything else. So, he was the mother too. I don't think anyone thought we would become anything, just live and die in that shitty council estate, but Kurt had ambitions and he was clever. Really clever, and he went off to university and became everything he dreamt of. He wanted to have everything we never had, a stable loving home. A mortgage. A yard. Stupid shit that is normal to most people, but we never had that, you know. Anyway, he got it. He got that job and he hated it, it sucked the life out of him, but I think he liked that. I think secretly he liked being that normal guy who hated his job but had a nice house in the suburbs. Then Marie left, and that was a huge blow. He wanted children; she wanted a husband that she actually saw. Both in completely different places in their heads."

She takes a deep sniffly breath, she is shaking now but not with the cold, and I do the only thing that I can do; I squeeze her hand a little tighter, she gives a muffled laugh and a sad smile as she squeezes back.

"When they finished him, he hit rock bottom. I told him, I told him he would find another job. That it was just a job, I could help him with money if he needed it. But he said he was fine. That he didn't need any help. He was the big one, the one who took care of me... So, me, carefree Lily took him at his word. But he wasn't fine. He wasn't fine at all, his demons ate away at him. Day and night, he was always strong, always taking care of everyone, but his thoughts had always had a dark edge and he was left alone with them. Marie tells herself it was an accident; he was drunk and just took too many. But I know Kurt better than anyone. It wasn't an accident, he did it on purpose, he wanted to die. I have learnt how to accept that. Actually, knowing it is what he wanted somehow makes it easier for me."

I stop and pull her tight against me. She is crying, but it is like she doesn't even know it. Just soft silent tears running down her cheeks in a steady stream until they drip from her chin. She is trembling and whilst she is a hurricane of a woman, fierce in more ways than I could list, she is fragile too, a little piece of her broken.

"I am sorry, Lily. Really. I am so sorry." I feel her tense in my arms and give herself a little shake, a mental note of pulling herself together.

"I am not sorry," she says as she pulls back, and I see that fiery steel in her eyes. "I am fucking furious. I cannot control the anger I feel. I hate them. I hate them all."

"Hate who, Lily? I don't understand." She gives me a wry smile, and with her fierce look and tear-streaked face she looks more formidable than I have ever seen her.

"Those bastards that did it to him. They didn't push him over the edge... they flung him off and they didn't care what happened to him when they let go. My brother, he was an investment banker."

And everything slowly starts to click into place.

7

I spend the night with Lily, she is emotional and on edge, and I feel like leaving her would be the worst thing I could do right now after she has shared so much with me. I turn off the job, the police side of my brain, and whereas usually that would be almost impossible for me, with Lily, I find it easy.

I don't need to dive into background research right now. I don't need to know every detail of her brother's death, of Lily's course of action after her brother's death. Later, I will trace and track her every move. I will go through the last few months with a fine-tooth comb and I will find the answers I need to paint the full picture.

My priority at that moment is giving Lily something she hasn't felt in a long time. Warmth, care, someone to hold her so she can start to let go of the anger she has been carrying like a burning ball of heated rage. She stripped herself of any comfort, detached herself from a life she knew and loved and then started her own crusade in some warped view of justice. I can almost understand it; her crimes are faceless, there are no victims, no single person paying the price. Just one big *fuck you* to the industry, to the ones who she feels tossed her brother aside and made him feel so useless and alone that he took his own life.

She said she wasn't angry at her brother, but I wonder to myself if she was being entirely truthful. Not with me, I think she is telling me what she thinks is the truth, but if she were to be truly honest with herself and look inside, I think she would find that some of this rage is for her brother, for him leaving her behind.

I don't know much about grief after the

initial phases. I have never experienced the kind of loss Lily has. My grandparents have passed away, but, in all cases, it was expected. There was illness, and a sad acceptance, the reality of old age that had made the loss easier to bear.

In the job, though, that is a different thing. I have seen death close up, so close I could taste it on my tongue. I've had to be the person to tell mothers, fathers, husbands and wives that their loved ones are gone. Watching that pain unfold, seeing worlds shatter... it is heartbreaking. Those first few moments, hours and days there is a numbness, but after, as I have worked with families through the case, through court, you see the numb fade away and the wound bleeds until there is nothing left to give. Only then does any kind of healing start, but I don't think they are ever really the same after. Like Lily said, there is always a before and an after.

But I don't believe this path she has started on is her after. Knowing now what I do and knowing the person she is inside, I know that once she finds a way to stop the bleeding, she will want to get off this train that is on a high-speed collision course. The only question that really remains is whether she is already too far down the track to avoid the crash.

That will depend on the people she has gotten herself mixed up with and what she is prepared to do to get herself out of the situation. I realise that I have already made my mind up that I will try to help her; I just am not sure how I can do that without telling her who I really am. And the weight of who I really am feels like lead around my neck. I feel guilty that she has shared her darkest hour with me and I haven't shared my secrets, but she stopped her story early too.

She hasn't explained who Spenn is or that her revenge is in the form of Bank Robber Girl. She hasn't mentioned that her new freelance work involves being a technical criminal genius and breaking into banks. So, my guilt isn't exactly overwhelming in that sense, but in another way, it is eating me up inside.

And when I think about Josh, I feel that

wave of panic. He will be so disappointed in me if he knows what I have done. How much I have risked for sex. I think perhaps he knows I am fucking her. We all know how undercover sometimes works. You do whatever it takes, but that part isn't spoken about back in the office. What he doesn't know is that I'm doing it because I want to, because I want her, and not just sexually and I cannot resist anything about her.

The truth is, he would see it as me risking everything for sex, but I think from the very first moment I met Lily I knew there was something more. It is so different with her than anything I have ever known. She captivated me from the very first second and now I have no idea how I am going to get her out of this mess. How the hell do I tell her who I really am?

SHE MURMURS as I slide out of her bed. I am sleeping in later and later. Pulling on my running gear, I bend over and fasten my laces.

"Will you be back?" she whispers sleepily. I come back over to her, brushing messy curls from her face as I kiss her forehead. Her long dark eyelashes flicker. "As soon as I can," I say softly and then I leave the apartment, breaking into a slow jog as I make my way to the city park.

I see Josh the second I turn into the gates of the park, and it only takes a second more for me to know that something is wrong. His body language is stiff, colder, more rigid. The moment he sees me, he looks away, our eyes not meeting, and he begins a slow jog away making me speed up to catch up with him.

"You said you had information for me?" His words are not cold but they are direct, curt. The tone he uses when he is being DS Cole and not Josh. I try not to feel affronted, but my tone also cools from my usual warm tone with him.

"Yes, I wanted to bring you up to date. I think you need to head back to Lily's brother. She told me that his death was the catalyst of her anger and that he was a banker. It was definitely the trigger point and I think it would provide more information on this ring she has got herself caught up in if we know where to trace it back to."

He nods. "I will get a team on it. The case has been opened up a little more now. More resources, it was authorized last night so we have had more eyes on to keep tails on all leads. We have the shop covered all the time. The tech guys are hesitant with Lily, they know how good she is. They are not sure what firewalls and encryptions she has in place, and they don't want to give her any warnings. They are relying on the others and then, of course, you."

He quietens off and the words sink in. I know what has happened. There are more people watching us, and they aren't naive. They know that when you're undercover you do whatever it takes. Have they seen shadows of us fucking through her big bay window and thin curtains? Have they seen my tenderness towards her? Do they know how deeply I have been drawn in? We are, of course, not supposed to fuck the suspects and if boundaries are breached, we are to report it immediately so it can be mitigated against should it go to trial, but if you report it you can be sure you will be benched from undercover ops for the foreseeable future. Nobody ever reports these things.

"Look, Frankie," he starts off, and his tone is still the same. Then he pauses and softens, "Look, it happens. We know it, and I know that you're an amazing operative. But you have to let me in here. Whether that's as your boss or your friend right now, I will take it, but if you lie to me and shut me out... I will have to put the department first."

I take a deep breath.

"Josh..." And so, I begin.

It takes me thirty minutes to tell him everything and I don't leave out any details. From the first moment I met her to the beginning of her heartfelt confessions last night. I talk to him as my best friend, explain the way she makes me feel. How I can't stop thinking about her and that I am so worried now about her future and how she doesn't seem to realize or perhaps even care about the kind of trouble she is in.

He is quiet and just listens to me and the heavy pad of our footprints as we make our way around the park again and again. I am not even breathless, and neither is he. I notice his looks leaner, fitter. He sees me look and gives me a wry grin.

"I come even on the days you're not here now. I kind of like it. Makes me feel better, ready for the day. Not saying I am going to be as committed as you, but I do like it."

"I told you it is therapeutic!" I exclaim, and he laughs.

"Yeah, and Sarah is a *big* fan of how my body is changing."

"Far too much information." I wince and he laughs harder. "What am I going to do, Josh?"

He nods towards a bench and we make our way over. I sit down with a heavy sigh.

"If I am honest, Frankie, it is a little out of your hands in many ways. I know and I understand why Lily feels the way she does. Fucking hell, I hate bankers too half the time, and her crime is faceless, there is no visible victim, but there will be victims. Just because you cannot see them or touch them doesn't mean they aren't there, maybe they won't reopen one of the branches again and then people will lose their jobs.

These big banks, they have a way of making sure that the people high up the chain don't pay for anything, it is always people like me, you, her brother who pay the price, and Lily is a contributing factor to that."

"I know that, Josh, and it doesn't matter if they reopen as normal, my view on the law hasn't changed in that I don't think she has broken it, or that her crimes can be excused. I just don't think she is seeing clearly or at least doesn't grasp the consequences."

"Then this is what you need to do. You need to get her to come in off her own back. She needs to switch sides and tell us everything then we can protect her. It is her only way out. It is the only way you can escape the mess you have both gotten into. There have been whisperings from above that if she wanted to apply her unique skillset for the good of this country, then exceptions could be made. The Chief will be happy. We get the others for the robberies. She is brilliant and the kind of person whose skills that are highly useful if we can transfer them to be used for forces of good. A win for the station, a huge win for the department with splashy arrests, a raid on a dodgy betting shop and Lily will escape with no real punishment other than the fact that she has had to betray the people she is working with. Do you think you can persuade her? Get her to come in?"

I know he is being my friend, but he is also working me too. He is pushing me to do the right thing for myself but also the job, and I respect that. His offer is not lost either, to offer Lily immunity to testify and to give information on how she is entering the bank servers is a huge thing. Many would not be so inclined to offer it to her, especially when we are right on the cusp of catching her anyway, but Lily is valuable and I have no doubt the police would love to have her. But, I think this offer is from higher than just the police. It has MI5 National Security Services written all over it. Someone of Lily's talent- I think MI5 want her and I think that is where this offer has come from.

"Okay, but first I need to get her to tell me the truth. All of it, and then I can try and get her to do the right thing."

He reaches over and takes my hand, giving it a soft squeeze. "As your boss, I hope you convince her for the sake of the department. But as your friend... I hope you do it so you can have some happiness. You deserve that, Frankie. If this Latte Collision Girl really is everything you say she is, I want you to have your chance with her."

I try to smile back at him, but the sad truth is that I don't feel hopeful.

ON MY WAY back to Lily's I stop off in the supermarket and pick up some things for breakfast and the newspapers catch my eye. Of course, they are still talking about the robbery- it is front-page news. An idea slots into place and I grab one along with the juice and eggs and meander back to Lily's apartment.

I took a key so I could let myself back in and don't need to wake her. Not that it matters, as I open the front door the curtains are wide open and Lily is at her computer. She doesn't rush to close things but she doesn't need to, because what I can see makes no sense to me anyway. Walking over to her, I kiss her softly at her neck and she tilts her head to one side offering me more of her pale soft skin to nibble and lick.

"I missed you," she moans lightly with a soft sigh.

"I missed you too, but I have got to get in the shower. Then I am making us breakfast." She tilts her head backwards so I get a glimpse of her wide grin.

"How did I get so lucky?" She beams, and I steal a kiss from her soft pink lips.

"I was just thinking the same."

I take a long, slow shower and I put my head into work mode. I know it is going to take all the skills I have and more to get Lily to open up and then persuade her. I think through possible scenarios, switch back into old Frankie, detective Frankie and mentally prepare myself.

Making my way into the kitchen I start hunting for the things I need. Lily is still working away on her computer, but I can't see her screen from this angle anyway. As the eggs start to cook, I casually open the paper on the countertop.

"Have you been following these robberies?" My tone is neutral, inexpressive, and I flip the eggs.

"Hmmm?" Lily questions nonchalantly. "The robberies..." I turn, holding up the paper. "Have you been following them?"

"Oh... those. Well yes and no. I don't follow it exactly but they are hard to get away from. It is all over everywhere."

"That's true. Everyone was talking about in the supermarket this morning. It's scary when you think about it. It makes me feel uneasy."

"What?" Lily turns in her chair and looks straight at me. "Why would you feel uneasy?"

I turn back to the eggs, which are starting to spit. "Well, they don't know who it is, how they are getting in there. I heard they are using software, maybe they will steal our details. They could blackmail people. And what are they using all of that money for? I bet its criminal stuff. I don't know, I just don't like it. I hope it ends soon."

I feel her arms slide slowly around my waist and she pulls me back against her. "You don't need to worry about that. You never need to worry about that," she whispers softly and I feel myself tremble.

"Of course I do, Lily, and you do too. We don't live in Robin Hood land. People who rob banks are serious criminals. We should definitely be careful."

"Honestly, you don't need to worry. It isn't anything like that. Your information is totally safe and if anything it will be safer now as they will have to try and get better security in the future to actually protect people."

"Oh yeah..." I ask softly, "How do you know that?"

I feel the pause, her hands stilling, her breath held. Maybe I am doing the same thing too, and then she answers low, soft, barely a whisper, "I know because I am the one getting into the servers."

I tense. My hands freeze and her palms tighten on my hips spinning me around to look at her.

"I wanted to tell you last night," she says earnestly, her eyes wide and full of worry. "But I didn't know how and I figured you might leave or hate me, but I don't want you to be worried. I hate that you're afraid. I didn't know that. I am sorry."

"Lily..." She steps back, giving me some space, and I realize that I need it. I oddly stumble over to the table and fall into the chair. "... I don't understand."

She turns the gas off and then comes to me. Sitting at the table she leans across and tries to take my hands in hers, but I pull them back out of her grasp. It kills me to be this way with her, but it is her only chance, our only chance. I have to get her into the station to confess.

"Please, please don't be like that," she begs softly.

"You have to tell me, Lily. Tell me what on earth happened."

"Oh Fran, I wish I had never started but I was so fucking angry. I knew how to get into the servers, how to cause issues for the banks. From an early age, I have absorbed myself in computers. I can hack any system now. Literally any computer system you can think of. I can find out anything. It is easy to me. But everything I did... they just covered it up. No one knew, it was like it didn't matter. I lost them millions and not a word was said. So, I thought about what will hit them the most. Humiliation. I found Spenn by doing some research. He had the means of doing the job once we were in. I could get us in. It was perfect. Except now... It isn't so hard to stop, not from my side. I want to stop. In the beginning, it made me feel invincible, it was addictive and I loved seeing them scramble. But now the thrill has gone. I don't feel good about it, but Spencer... Well, he isn't exactly the kind of guy that is easy to say no to. I have told him, one more. Just one more, but he probably won't listen. I don't know. It is a mess."

"It isn't a mess, Lily. It is right and wrong. I know how you feel, and I understand your anger and your pain." I slide my hands slowly over the table and take hers in mine. "But you are not a bad person, I know that. And whilst it seems like no one is hurting, trust me it will be normal people like you and me that will pay the price for those robberies. No one else. It has to stop."

I watch a big fat tear run down her face. She gives me a little nod, along with a sniffle.

"I know, but, how can I? What can I do?

You saw Spenn turn up here when I didn't reply to him. It is easy money for him. I can get him in anywhere. He won't let me just stop."

"The only thing you can do, the only right thing to do, is to go to the police. Tell them everything, and then help them stop Spencer. That way you won't get in more trouble and it will all come to an end. Plus, it sounds like this Spenn is a dangerous guy, he needs to be off the streets."

Her eyes get a little frantic; I can see she is afraid, but it only makes me hold on tighter.

"You can help them. You have something that they need, information. Use it to get what you need, and out of this mess. It might not be easy, but it is the right thing, Lily. I promise."

She takes a hard swallow and a long deep breath. Giving me a small nod that grows more and more determined.

"Okay. But will you come with me?"

My turn for a deep breath. "Of course."

AT THE NEXT chance I get, I message Josh and tell him that Lily and I will be coming into the station. He will make all the necessary arrangements but going as late as possible when there is less staff around will be the less likely it is for my cover to be blown. Normally I would take her to a different station, but I only trust Josh to give Lily the deal she needs to ensure that she won't be prosecuted. So, I have to take the risk.

My heart is racing, Lily and I talk through the situation a few times. She practices explaining the facts, what she can do for them and what she wants in return. Her voice gets a little stronger and clearer each time.

"What if they arrest me now? What if I go to jail? What if I can't come home? Will you take care of things here for me?"

"It isn't going to come to that, Lily, okay? It is going to be okay. Just please don't worry."

"Promise me though? Promise if they don't let me out that you'll take care of my things."

I put my arm around her as we walk down the street, pulling her closer to me, I feel her warmth against my body and I feel her tremble too. "I promise," I whisper softly as I lead us both into the station and into the hands of fate.

"I love you," she whispers almost silently into my shoulder. I pretend not to hear the words.

8

I watch as Josh unpeels the wrappers from the cassette tapes and slips them into the recorder.

"Lily, this interview will be recorded, you will hear a beep when I press record. Do you object to the recording of this interview?"

"No," Lily says softly and Josh nods and clicks the record.

"'This interview is being audio recorded. This is an interview with... state your full name, please." Josh pauses at the relevant parts to allow Lily to answer. "State your address please...." "State your date of birth, please..."

"I am DS Cole, badge number 65247. Also present is DI Roland, badge number 98647, and for your comfort, your friend, Fran Edmonds is accompanying you. There are no other persons present. The date is October 24th . The time is 18.32. We are in an interview room at Compton Street Police Station. At the conclusion of the interview, I will give you a form that will explain the procedure for dealing with this recording and how you can have access to it."

"Lily Archer, you do not have to say anything. But it may harm your defence if you do not mention when questioned something which you later rely on in court. Anything you do say may be given in evidence. I am going to ask you some questions. You do not have to answer any of them unless you want to. But if you go to court and say something there which you have not told me about, and they think you could have told me, it may harm your case. Anything you do say may be repeated in court. Do you understand, Lily?"

Lily nods, and I nearly tell her but stop myself.

"For the purposes of the tape, Lily, I will need you to answer out loud," Josh says with a reassuring smile. Lily clears her throat.

"Yes, I understand."

"'I must ask you why you have not requested legal advice or to consult with a legal representative. I must remind you that you can ask at any time for free legal advice during the course of this interview. If you want legal advice, say so and I will suspend the interview and arrange for legal representation. Do you understand?"

"Yes, I understand."

"Are you prepared to continue and answer questions without legal representation at this time?"

"Yes." She is brave and she looks boldly ahead. She knows it is highly likely she will go to jail for what she has done, but she continues anyway.

"Okay, Lily. I am going to ask you now a few questions and then we are going to talk about what can happen next okay?"

I squeeze her hand hard under the table, she gives herself a little shake and sits up taller in her chair. Those beautiful blue eyes flash with the steely confidence I know and love, and I smile at her.

"I am ready."

And so it begins.

~

Lily is brave and unwavering. She talks clearly, slowly, and Josh guides her, like the professional he is, digging out the details. He breaks the interview and leaves the room. When he returns, he advises Lily should take council and I should wait outside.

I know it is the best advice, they are going to offer her a deal and she needs to be sure that it protects her. As much as I can answer that for her, it isn't my place and would, in fact, negate the legalities of the deal should I be there. But it is still hard to walk away and leave her alone in the interview rooms. Her lawyer arrives shortly and I sit and watch the clock tick by.

It seems to take forever, but in reality, it is only a couple of hours, heading into the night, yet I feel completely awake as the lawyer walks past me with Lily in tow.

I stand and she crashes against me, pulling me close, and I feel her stress, anxiety, tension all seeping away as I hold her tight. I look over my shoulder at Josh who gives me a short nod and then turns and leaves.

"See, I told you, you would be going home," I say with a teary smile, emotions taking over me. She smiles back while taking my hand, our fingers lacing together. "We are going home, together," she replies. She leads me out of the station.

"It isn't over yet," she begins to explain as we make our way down the station steps. "There is a deal I have signed that protects me from prosecution. Ultimately, I haven't taken any of the money myself. They brought in an agent from the Security Services, MI5. They want me to work for them. MI5. Well, I will work for them after all this. But they need to catch Spenn and the others in action, so I have to rob one more bank. I thought it might be over now. But it isn't. I need to lie to them... I'll be betraying them... I'm not the best liar."

"Frankie! I almost didn't see you there!" A figure entering the station calls out to me,

"DS just called us all into work, congrats on the scoop. You must be buzzing!"

I freeze.

It takes a few seconds for Lily's sentence to trail off, for the pieces to come together. As my hand tightens rigidly around her fingers, I feel hers go slack. She looks from me to DI Stevenson. He too seems to be putting the pieces together, and I see the look of apology as he walks past me and into the station without saying another word.

I close my eyes for a second, my heart in my chest, then when I open them Lily is pulling her hand from my grip. Her blue eyes blazing so bright but I see the shimmer of angry tears.

"You... You..." Shock. She is in complete shock, barely able to put her words together. "You have been lying to me all this time? I trusted you. Fuck. To get me to... Fuck. Fuck. I can't believe you could do this. I can't believe..." She starts to step backwards, moving away from me, she is shaking with anger. Pain spills from her words and tears run down her cheeks, but it is her anger that wins.

"Lily, please, please listen to me. It isn't

what you think." I move forwards, starting to beg, pleading for her to understand. "It hasn't been a lie. I promise you."

"Are you a police officer?" she asks me directly, coldly, folding her arms in front of her with a steely resolve. "Are you?" she says louder.

"Yes, but my feelings for you are real. I swear I've fallen in love with you." The moment I say it, I know it is true and it makes her pause, for a second. And then she says calmly, sadly,

"I really thought I loved you... But now... I don't even fucking know you." She spits the words. Her blue eyes blaze into mine.

Then she turns and walks slowly away and out of my life.

9

I don't know how I make it home that night. It is all a blur, and the days after pass in a numb haze. I don't know what day it even is anymore, what I should be doing.

My cover is blown so I am back in the station. Everyone keeps congratulating me for my side of the operation, though it is not quite over yet. Lily still has one last task to perform, although she now has a case handler and works directly with them. Josh asked me if I wanted to continue with the operation and be part of the sting, but I decided that it was for the best for me to just step away.

Lily made her feelings perfectly clear, to him, not me. She told him under no uncertain terms was I to be around her, that she would do as agreed and keep to her end of the deal, but she would not be in my company.

He tells me, quite politely, what she said to him. I can picture her face, imagine her tone, know her anger, and even his calmness does nothing to quell my pain.

It was bound to happen, there was no other way in the end. She was always going to find out who I was, that I had lied to her. But maybe in time I could have found a way to tell her myself, softened the blow, showed her with love and affection the truth, proved to her that since the moment I met her there was something more there than just working her as a source.

But the opportunity was torn from me and I now have to live with the consequences.

I can't believe how much it hurts; I haven't known her long really, but she touched every part of my life in a way I can't begin to describe. Now, imaging a future without her in it... I just feel this cloud of darkness hanging over me. I know Josh is worried, and can visibly see the changes in me, both mentally and physically. I can't eat, I can't sleep, I am just in a fog of constant pain.

I hate that I have lost her. I hate even more that I have hurt her. She has no-one. She thought she could trust me and I betrayed her.

"DC Miller!" I hear my name called louder and I turn. "Hmmm?" I ask. Josh is looking over at me with worry. "My office." I stand up and make my way over. I hear the whispers. I know the others can't understand it, why I am not celebrating one of the biggest achievements in my career, but I don't care what they think or even what the rumours are. I slip into Josh's office and close the door behind me.

"You wanted to see me, Sarge?" I ask quietly.

"Fucking hell, Frankie, yes I wanted to see you. Sit down, please." He wafts his hand at the empty chair and I park myself in it, barely looking up at him.

"Look, I have tried my best but there is nothing that can be done. The operation is tomorrow night and I know you wanted to respect Lily's request, but the truth of the matter is that the chief wants you involved because you know her best, know how she thinks and will know how to keep her safe if, and this is huge if, but if anything goes wrong. I have thought long and hard about it and I think he is right."

I am not surprised because it is the smart answer. Even in an advisory capacity here in an op room I can be of some value. Lily's wishes will be noted, but her safety is now the priority and so noted or not makes no difference; if the department feels I should be involved. I will be involved.

I let out a little sigh.

"I get it. I will be here."

"The thing is though, Frankie, I need you *here*, here. Not just physically but with your brain on, I need you alert. Lily is working with some serious criminals who know that she is looking for the exit door. They are going to be watching her like a hawk, and we need to keep her safe. They will not think twice about killing her if they think she has double crossed them. We know that they will be carrying guns. It only takes a second to shoot someone. That means you need to be watching every detail."

I sigh loudly. "I know, Josh. I won't let you down and I won't let anything happen to her." I look him straight in the eye so he can trust in what I am saying because it is the truth. He holds my gaze for a moment, and I feel his eyes bore into mine, and then he nods.

"Okay. Go home, eat, run, shower, sleep because you look like shit and we have a long day tomorrow."

I take a deep breath and give him a nod standing slowly. "I will be *here*, here."

I FOLLOW his advice and stop off at the store on the way home and buy myself the biggest, cheesiest pizza on the shelf. Tossing it in the oven when I get in, I pull out my phone.

I haven't messaged or called Lily, I have tried to respect her want for me to stay away, but I know she will be alone and nervous about tomorrow. I send a message.

I am thinking of you. I am around, if you want to talk F x x

I wait and watch but even though it sends from my side, I don't get the delivered message. I knew it was possible she would block me, but it still comes like a knife in my side. To know she hates me that much she couldn't even stand to see my name on her phone.

I think crazy thoughts. Maybe I should go round there. Maybe I should just see her and tell her how I feel, try and explain. But even as my mind races with the possibility I know that I won't.

I was so stupid; I knew she was different and I invaded her world. I let her open herself up to me in a way that I didn't deserve—emotionally, physically and all in between. I knew how fragile she was. I had known the truth, knew where we would end, but she had had no idea. When I had taken her to the police and they had offered her a lifeline, she felt a peace, a chance at a future for us together and then in a split second it had all been taken from her as she saw me for who I really was: a liar.

I don't deserve her forgiveness; I didn't deserve her trust. I smell burning and pull the pizza out of the oven. It is still edible, just. If I avoid the edges. Then I sit there on my kitchen floor, picking off burnt cheese as fat salty tears roll down my cheeks and the sharp pain of loss cuts through my very soul.

THE STATION IS alive with the buzz of an operation. If you aren't on the inside you are envious because those tingles of wrapping up an investigation are what we live for. Even me, still not slept and feeling like I am living in a constant fog, can't help but feel the atmosphere.

I make my way into the briefing room where the plan is laid out. The boards are covered in tacks, post-it notes and pins. Photos with cords connecting them, timelines, plans and layouts of the branch, streets and roads that web out around it. To the untrained eye it may look chaotic, a mess, but to me it is a clear illustration of a thorough and carefully planned operation;

I can see Josh buzzing with adrenaline inside and as if on cue, he begins.

"Okay, listen up everyone. We're in for a quiet afternoon of observation. The reason why we haven't been able to catch a break on this is due to the simplicity of the operation. Lily will make her way to the betting shop at 9 pm where she usually waits for a couple of hours doing her last-minute security checks." Josh makes his way over to the board where a map of the area is pinned. He points to the blue dot, which I know is Lily's home and then the red, which is the betting shop. I think for a second about Lily's home. The warmth of her huge comfy bed, the beautiful way the whole space fills with light from the big windows, the simplicity of it's open plan world. So very Lily. Then I shake myself out of it. *Focus, Frankie. For fuck's sake.*

"It is from here the van will pick them up. She doesn't know anything about the vehicle only that it has been different each time and that it is Spencer and his crew who source it. At this point they make their way directly to the target bank, which tonight will be..." He takes a yellow sticker and places it on the map. "The National Bank on Kent Street. It isn't the best location, but it was the one already chosen before we stepped in and it is too much of a risk to try to change it now."

I sit forwards and look at the location. It isn't ideal, a few exits point off the street, alleyways and places to run by foot. Josh looks around the room making sure we all have eyes on the board before he continues.

"Lily has been instructed to make a getaway along with the rest of them if it comes to that. She is wearing a tracker, we will find her, but if anything goes wrong, we don't want her actions to look suspect and make her a target later on. So, if you are the ground team and you're the one to make her arrest, for Christ sake make it look real but remember she is on our side."

I nod and smile to myself; she will play her part perfectly, that I am certain of.

"Now, we are going to have four ground teams in operation. Team one and two will be covering off the main road at either side in vehicles. They will be there solely for the purpose of if they manage to get back in their own vehicle. Teams three and four will be on foot. Team three will be the first team to engage the moment the suspects enter the bank. I am hoping that we can make all the arrests there and then, but we will also have Team four stationed a little further back covering off all the exit points along the street until we reach Team one and two. Okay, is everyone on the same page?"

"Yes, Sarge," we all reply almost in unison.

"Great, now the lists are up for which Team you will be part of and who is the responsible officer for each, plus your comms channel. Don't forget we will have a full team here to work on everything. We're going to CCTV tag each member as they exit the van so we should know exactly where each of them is at all times. Right, let's do our job!"

I wait for the hustle of everyone else making their way to the boards before I saunter over, knowing I will be in the operation room here, but as I glance over the list, I don't see my name. I glance across at the others and there I am, top of Ops three as the reporting Inspector.

"What the... ?" I murmur.

"Ahh, DC Miller, I saw you were assigned Operations Room by DS Cole but I thought after all the hard work you have put in on the case you deserved nothing less than the heading up the operation on foot."

"Th-thanks, Sir," I stutter as the DSU gives me a smile before leaving. It is the kind of thing I had dreamt of; these kinds of opportunities are what move you up the ranks. It would make the difference between a promotion or staying a DC, and that is a huge deal. It also means I will be closer to Lily too. I will be able to look out for her. I know she doesn't want that, but she will never know; I can just lead the team and watch from the frontline to make sure she gets out of the fray and into safe hands. I see Josh is looking over at me and he raises his eyebrows as if to check if I am okay. I give him a sharp, determined nod; I am okay and I am ready. I can do this.

10

The afternoon drags. Josh was right. The gang run a smooth operation; there is no last-minute panic or mad dash. The betting shop runs as it does every single day we have watched. The only difference in the routine is that at 9 pm, like clockwork, Lily leaves her apartment and makes her way there. I watch her as I strap myself into my stab vest, checking my comms, memorising the layout of the side streets around the bank and prepare to head outside.

She walks with her normal sway, her boots almost dancing along the pavement and her long warm cardigan pulled tight around her. Her hair is loose in her wild style that looks windswept even when there is no wind to be seen and it is so her and for a second I feel a physical ache to touch her, to hold her, to kiss her.

I take a deep breath and shake myself and head out of the room, out of the station, and jump into the van.

My instincts take over from this point. It isn't the first time I have led an operation, and I have a good team with me. They listen to my instructions avidly and when I ask for confirmations, they reaffirm the course of action perfectly. We are parked one street over from the bank, waiting.

For now, all we can do is wait, but the moment they leave the betting shop is when my heart begins to pound. They will get here in around four minutes. At that point, we know they run a clean enter-exit plan with one member remaining in the vehicle.

Lily has confirmed they work on a maximum of five minutes once they have entered the bank before they are leaving. So that is how long we have to detain the driver. Put the van out of action and arrest the rest. It is a short window with a few moving parts and we want to be as quiet as we can so we don't alert them inside, but I know we can do it.

Our countdown begins and we make our way out of the van. Spenn chooses this time of the night so he can hide from the CCTV and there is a low chance of any passers-by seeing them, it has worked in his favour for weeks. He has used the cover of darkness to aid him in going undetected. Well, tonight we will use it to our advantage.

We are already near enough in position as the van pulls up. I see them exit the van, I know the second Lily's boot slips out of the door that it is her, and she does her work effortlessly. The bank door clicks open as though she has a key and they enter.

I have the Ops Room in my ear, but I can see clearly for myself what is happening. I signal to the team and we make our way around the van. I hear the soft *psstz* noise as the tyres are slashed. Making a U formation around the front of the bank we get into our positions. All of us know what we need to do.

Five minutes seems like no time at all but waiting with one knee digging into the gravelly high street, my eyes unblinkingly staring at the door, it feels like a lifetime. They move with stealth that I almost admire. Even being this close to the entrance I can barely see any movement inside the bank and hear no noise.

"*Team one in position.*" I hear in my earpiece followed by, "*Team two in position.*"

I check around my team then I murmur softly in response, "Team three in position." And I hear the final reply of, "*Team four in position.*"

The door clicks in response, the first figure to leave is Lily and she moves off to the side; she knows we are there, but she does her best not to look for us in the shadows. I count them off... one... two... three... and finally the fourth leaves- the door closing behind them.

"Stop! Nobody Move!" I yell at the top of my lungs as the street lights up, the officers behind me flick on the full beams and the suspects freeze in surprised panic. Then comes the chaos. Of course, they don't stop, they scatter; no longer standing still like rabbits caught in the headlights. It is pure instinct, fight or flight, and at this moment, running seems like a good option to them. I see Lily's shock momentarily at my voice. The ones that can, jump into the van. Not Lily, she is too far ahead and I see it happening in slow motion.

The driver, unaware that we silently took out the tyres, turns on the ignition and puts his foot to the floor with a rev.

"Nooooo!" I scream, moving, running, racing forwards, but it is too late. The vehicle shudders into life and lurches forwards only to skid off track as the tyres give way. Lily has nearly crossed the front of the bonnet... but not quite.

The front bumper catches her legs and her slim frame lithe in tight black clothing, is propelled upwards, she rides over the white paintwork of the van, before spinning off the side and into the road. I hear the scream from her lips and then the crack of her head against the ground and then silence. Her body is still and unmoving.

Around me, I hear the voices of the officers, "You are under arrest on suspicion of bank robbery... You do not have to say anything... but it may harm your defence if you do not mention when questioned something which you later rely on in court... Anything you do say may be given in evidence."

I hear the words but I can't focus on them, knocking them out of the way, the vehicle continues before swerving and skidding to a halt. The other officers close in, pulling the suspects out, arresting them.

But I only see Lily.

I fall beside her, aware of all of my training. I don't move her head, only gently pulling up her black balaclava so I can check her lips for a sign of breathing. My fingers tremble as I take her wrist, feeling for a pulse as my cheek hovers about her mouth. That tiny little thud against my fingers fills my heart with joy. And as I hover close to her lips, I see her eyes begin to flicker. There is blood beginning to ooze on her forehead under her balaclava.

"Lily... Lily, sweetheart, can you hear me. Don't move just listen to me... I need you to stay with me, okay? Keep your eyes open... look at me, Lily... can you hear me? Lily... Lily!" I watch her eyes come in and out of focus and I feel hands on me trying to pull me away.

"No! No!" I scream, wrestling against the strong grip. "Frankie, Frankie! It's me. It's Josh, you have to move away. You have to let them in, let them do their job. Frankie, come on... Let the paramedics in."

My body goes limp and I watch the paramedics descend on her, moving slowly but working as a team. "How could this happen?" I whisper as tears roll in thick heavy tears down my face. They slide the stretcher underneath her and slowly pick her up. She is so tiny, thin, frail—it takes no effort.

"Go with her," Josh says to me and I feel his arms loosen around me, letting me go. I follow the stretcher, hopping up into the ambulance, and I watch as they start to get her stable. In my job I am used to these kinds of scenes, the IVs going in, the beep of the monitors, the rushed and yet calm conversations.

Lily slips in and out of consciousness. I ask the paramedic closest to me if I can hold her hand and he nods with a small smile. "Talk to her too, it will help keep her focusing, we need to keep her awake as long as we can until she has her CT scan." I nod and squeeze her hand a little tighter, even now her skin is warm in my palm.

"Lily? Lily lovely, you have to stay awake a little longer, darling," I say softly, moving in closer to her. Her eyes are open, just, but I can see they are filled with worry, anxiety, shock. "It is going to be okay; we are nearly at the hospital and they are going to take great care of you, okay? I won't let anything happen to you; I promise. You are going to be just fine." I feel the tiniest of squeezes and my heart bursts with love for this strong brave woman.

"See, you are going to be just fine," I reassure her and myself.

I SIT in the hospital canteen and nurse cup after cup of strong sludge-like coffee. As soon as my cup empties, I move to the machine and take another until I am shaking from the amount of caffeine I have surging through my veins. The hospital is quiet, the canteen itself closed, and only the vending machines provide any nourishment. The door opens every so often, other friends or family in blurry-eyed shock hunting down a distraction from their reality.

I don't know if a nurse will come and find me. I told them where I would be and as a detective, I can request information about a patient/suspect, however, I think it is clear to everyone that I am not here as a detective and Lily is not just a patient or a suspect.

My phone lights up on the table, but it is only Josh asking if there is any news. I don't bother to reply. There is no news, and it has been hours, so I have no idea if that is a good thing or not. I try not to let my mind focus on it. The worst-case scenarios hover and then fall on my shoulders like an immovable dead weight. Morning is here and daylight begins to fill the canteen. I feel like I am suffocating on air, every breath I take feels thick. I drain the cup, again, and stand slowly to take another refill when the door swings open. Not a nurse, a doctor, and my heart sinks.

"DC Miller?" he asks.

"That's me, you can call me Frankie though." He gives me a curt nod.

"Okay, Frankie, Lily is out of surgery now and I have good news and bad news. The good news is that whilst she experienced a significant head wound, these things always look worse than they are and although there will be a scar we expect no lasting issues there. She also has fractured some ribs, which although painful, will heal."

I take a huge breath of relief. "Thank you, Doctor."

"Well, like I said there is some bad news. Her biggest issue a fractured tibia and fibula in her leg. We have inserted some metal work for her in surgery. She is going to need to undergo some serious physiotherapy and she won't have a speedy recovery. If she wants to walk as she did before, she will need to dedicate a lot of time and hard work to her rehabilitation. But she is young, otherwise healthy, and obviously a strong woman so I do believe a full recovery is possible. But she, and you, need to be prepared for the long road ahead. It isn't necessarily going to be a smooth ride."

"I don't know if I will be along for that ride, Doctor, but I do know if anyone has the strength to get through a full recovery it is Lily."

He frowns a little, his eyes furrowed as he looks me up and down. "Why aren't you sure if you will be there?"

I give a sad smile. "I think I am the last person Lily wants around her right now, but thank you for coming to tell me. I do appreciate that."

"Well, you are welcome but also I think mistaken. I am here only because Lily has woken up and the first thing she asked for is for me to come and fetch you, it would seem to me that she most definitely does want you around, DC Miller."

As I enter her private room, I try not to let my shock at her appearance show on my face. Her head is neatly bandaged, but strands of her hair are still matted with blood and a graze is prominent on her cheekbone. Her leg is set in a plaster cast and all of her body that I can see on her left side is covered in scratches, cuts and deep purple bruises that blossom across her skin.

She turns just a little to face me and even that slight movement elicits a small wince from her. I move slowly to her. My thick, heavy, police-issue boots seem to thud across the tiled floor, but it doesn't seem as loud as how hard and heavy my heart beats in my chest.

"I know… I look pretty bad." Her blue eyes twinkle as they reach mine, full of mischievous smiles that make the butterflies flutter in my stomach.

"No, you look beautiful." My reply comes without filter and I inch closer, still not quite sure of whether she wants me here. "How do you feel?"

"I feel woozy and uncomfortable. They hooked me up on some pretty good painkillers, but it is kind of surreal. Like I know that the pain is there, and it is hovering but I can't quite feel it yet. Which is a good feeling but then at the same time, I almost want to know how bad it is going to be. Is that weird?" she questions with a scrunch of her nose and I laugh.

"A little, but I understand the need to know. Then you can prepare."

"I don't think preparation has ever helped me. The only person who knew what was going to happen and yet I walked in front of a van... It wasn't my smartest move," she says with a wry smile. I take the chair and pull it up closer to her bed and then sit down on the edge of the hospital green leather.

"It wasn't the smartest move but to give you some credit, it wasn't moving when you first stepped out," I say reasonably, and she bursts into laughter and then clutches at her ribs with her right hand.

"Oh, Fran...Frankie, please don't make me laugh. I can't take it."

"Sorry," I mumble, and I look away. It kills me to see her in pain and to know the doctor is right. She has a long recovery ahead of her. I don't even know how she will make it up her stairs, never mind navigate life, alone.

"What are you thinking about?" she asks softly and I look to her.

"I am thinking about how sorry I am. How I wish I had done so many things differently. How worried I am about you. How proud I am of how brave you were, how brave you are. How much I have missed you. I know you didn't want me there, but I didn't have much of a choice. But seeing you, seeing that moment, I have never felt anything like it. I was screaming on the inside."

"You were screaming on the outside too," she replies with a soft smile. "I knew you would be there; I was just angry at you and I wanted to lash out. But I heard you, it was you in my head as I was spinning through the air. I thought if she is screaming like that, it must be bad. Imagine if that had been my last thought... You really need to work on that, Frankie," she says with a chuckle and I smile too.

"I am hoping you won't rob another bank again and then get hit by the getaway vehicle but just in case... Yes, I will work on it." She laughs harder and then winces but still continues to laugh.

I lean forwards, my hand reaching for her fingers, and she offers them. Her laughter subsides as I slowly, softly trace my fingertips up and down her small delicate fingers.

"Did it work? Did you get them all?" she asks, her voice light but I hear the subtle quiver of fear.

"Yes, the operation went perfectly in that respect. Everyone was arrested and is in custody. Plus, you know we had the extra CCTV installed in the bank so we have it all recorded. They will be put away for a long time and as far as they are concerned you are in custody too. They don't know what you did. As the agreement you signed states, you will be protected. As far as they are concerned you will be in jail for a long time too."

She visibly relaxes.

"How do you feel about the MI5 thing? We didn't really get chance to talk about that."

She shrugs a little.

"I feel good about it really. Excited actually. To be able to use my skills for good. I mean, the pay isn't exactly bank robber salary, but you know..."

I laugh. "Honestly, you are the only

person I know that would rob multiple banks and not even keep a pound."

"Well, you know, I didn't do it to for that, I don't even care about the money," she says quietly.

"I know." I let go of her hand. I feel her body stiffen, emotions surging as she battles with my betrayal. The wounds are there still and are not numbed by the painkillers. This pain is inside and I have caused it. "I would like to explain. If you want me to?" She doesn't say anything, just gives me a slight nod.

I have always found it hard to express my feelings. A wall that I don't try to scale, I have always preferred to leave things unsaid than to try and say how I truly feel, that way you can't get hurt. But I also know that if I don't put myself out there, if I don't tell Lily how I feel, I will lose her. And I can't lose her, well maybe I still will, but at least I can say that I tried. That I was honest and I told her how I felt. There can be no doubt then in her mind of my feelings for her. So, I take a long, deep breath and I tell her all the things I should have said before.

"The moment I saw you, that morning we crashed into each other in the coffee shop... I felt something. I was drawn to you but I had no idea who you were or anything. Then I went into work and I saw you on CCTV. Actually, I saw your boots, your star, and I just knew it was you. I don't know why I took the job; I think because I wanted to get closer to you. I wanted to know you, be part of your life. So, then I waited for you, and we met, and I just... I don't think it was ever about the job, other than wanting to protect you and keep you safe. It was all real. All of it. My feelings... I just had no control. I tried to keep a distance, but it was impossible with you. I fell in love with you straight away and in every way. I knew I would have to tell you eventually, and I know it seems as though I didn't protect my job or whatever, but my boss already knew. It wasn't that, I wanted to get you out of the mess... I wanted to find a way to help you. I didn't want you to fall in deeper with them or spend the next however many years in prison. So, I wanted to get through this and then tell you, and hope you would forgive me. I know I don't deserve it."

I look into her stunning blue eyes, mine pleading with hers to understand, to forgive me, to see how much I feel for her.

"Do you have a car?" she asks quietly.

"A car? Yes, why?" I asked, confused.

"Well, if what you are saying is true, you have a lot of making up to do." She smiles mischievously. "I mean, I can't exactly walk up to my apartment or around town, can I? I'll need you to drive me home. Also, it is a good job you are strong- you will need to carry me up the stairs." She bites her lip with a gentle nibble and my heart bursts for her.

"Do you mean it? You forgive me?" My voice is barely a whisper as I stand, moving towards the side of the bed as she nods. I cup her face and stoke her bruised cheek tenderly, wiping away her tears.

"You are all I can think about. When the van hit me... it was you. Only you. I love you, Frankie." I nod, not able to speak, words caught in my throat so I lower, ever so gently, and kiss her soft sweet lips.

The moment our lips meet I feel that

spark. Electricity zaps through me in a way that only happens with her, I tingle from head to toe, my heart pounding and pulse racing; I am dizzy in my love for her. She murmurs gently against my lips as my other hand moves and I lower, so carefully, not wanting to hurt her in any way but desperate to be close to her and wrapped up in her love and her warmth.

Everything is still complicated, but I can see a way through it and I can see the future for us.

"I have missed you," she whispers.

"I love you," I say.

"I love you too," she smiles.

"It feels like it has been forever," I reply.

"We have forever," she says softly, and she is absolutely right. We do.

EPILOGUE

Josh slides me an icy Bud across the countertop, which I accept gratefully by taking a long deep gulp. He gives me a cheeky grin and I respond with a frown.

"I did warn you that being a," He held his fingers up in air quotes, "'*Sarge*' is not all it's cracked up to be. I mean, yes, I loved it, but it is a lot of pressure. Especially when the DSU is a *reaaal* dick."

I flick my bottle cap at him, which hits him perfectly square on the chin.

"Good aim, Detective *Sergeant* Miller, good aim." He laughs and I groan.

"Ughhhh, what a week. When are they due back? I am starving and so ready to just drink all your beer and stuff my face with hot, cheesy pizza," I say as I slide forward over the counter. In response, he rolls his eyes.

"Like that is anything new and also how would I know how long they're going to take. You sent my wife off with your wife-to-be wedding dress shopping. It could be hours, days, weeks. All I hope is they have your card and not mine. Although I have already heard the words, *new hat,* so I am not sure how much that is going to cost me, but I figure the pay rise is needed."

I look up at him with an expression of incredulity. "You have to buy a hat... fuck me. I said a small wedding. We don't even know anyone! Next minute we have one hundred guests and a hall hired. Do you know that you can pay extra for glittered icing on your wedding cake? No, I didn't either, but there you go. She has wedding craziness, I can't even—"

"Can't even what, my love?" I feel small, soft hands run through my hair then give my curls a soft little tug. I try to keep my exasperated face, but it is no use. Josh rolls his eyes at my lack of resolve as I visibly melt at her touch. Turning in my chair, I slide my arms around her and bury myself in the nook of her neck, breathing in her scent as I line her neckline with light kisses.

"I can't even believe how lucky I am," I whisper, and Lily squeezes me tight. "Nice save," she giggles. "You are lucky because not only did I buy a dress but we bought pizza!" She grins and behind her, Sarah walks in with a ta-da, and I can smell the oozing cheesy goodness from here.

"So fucking lucky," I murmur back against her lips before giving them a ravenous bite.

WE DON'T STAY TOO long at Josh and Sarah's. We eat, drink, laugh and chat, but it only takes one glance at her watch and a subtle run of her fingers up my inner thigh and my mind is firmly focused on dessert—and not the chocolate kind. As we walk through the city, we cross at what we now call Lily's Street. It's been three years since she went spinning over the front of the van. I can still hear the crack of her head against the pavement. But I can also look back on the hard months that came after, where she pushed herself mentally and physically to recover.

It wasn't easy, don't get me wrong. There were many long nights, tears, days of dark depression where she could not do the things she wanted to do. There was also fear as the court case began; she was scared they wouldn't be prosecuted, that they would know she had turned, that they would come looking for her.

I think that she gave them too much credit, but I did understand the fear and I supported her in every way that I could. We watched the trial unfold in the comfort of my apartment. I took some time away from work, which they were more than happy to give me after the recent arrest and soon-to-be prosecution of the infamous bank robbers.

Because they *were* prosecuted and sentenced, two of them even took deals to do less time and incriminate Spenn and others in their network of crimes.

Everyone is happy. As for me, happy isn't even the word. It is a constant feeling of contentment, that sparks and glistens with love, lust, passion and desire. I wake in the morning and reach for her before my eyes open. My heart explodes when I hear her laugh, and in those moments where she is sad, when I see a hint of a tear, I feel like I could take on the world just to make her smile again.

Lily was nervous when she had recovered enough to get dragged into MI5 training school. They don't officially call them 'spies' but that is what she is. Lily is a spy working for her country.

I know the DSU was a bit perplexed with the arrangement, and I had a feeling he would try and pull the rug from under it pretty sharpish. But, unsurprisingly, it seems like MI5 hold the power to do exactly as they like. It became startlingly clear how much they wanted Lily and strings were pulled all over the place to make that happen. Lily could make computers do things that seemed to perplex even those that are specialists in the field. One computer guy once told me that coding should be written like an equation whereas Lily played it like a symphony. It shouldn't work, and yet the melody was perfect. I have long since stopped trying to understand in the slightest. All I know is that she soon thrived in her new job. It is anything but 9-5 and Lily loves that. It works for me too. I love what I do and we both get each other. We understand the demands of each other's work. We don't ask questions when the other is called out or away for weeks, or whatever. We just make the most of our time when we do have it, losing ourselves in each other.

Private contractors approached Lily in the wake of the arrests offering her a lot of money to work for them. Lily wasn't interested. "I have all I want," she said with a soft shrug and a small smile and dismissed them time after time.

After Lily's recovery, we decided it was better if she just moved in with me. There was a long list of practical reasons, but truth be told I couldn't stand the thought of her leaving. I didn't want to not go to bed with her, to not wake up with her, to not share the shower, to not steal her hairbands.

Any trepidation I had about living with someone again never materialised with Lily. It was like the idea of not living with her was just not even an option, and from that moment on our lives entwined in every single way. Josh was unsure for about five minutes; Lily was easy to like, and she and Sarah clicked instantly. Josh and I joked about their budding friendship, but I think we both secretly liked it. Especially for Sarah who had to endure hours and hours of work talk, she now had someone to roll her eyes with and to talk about things not work related.

Then a month ago we met at our café, we still go once a week for vanilla lattes, and I realised this was it for me. I didn't want anyone else, not now or ever. I regret the way I asked her, I wish I had made some big gesture, a moment for her to remember for the rest of her life. She deserved the movie moment, but instead I looked up at her over my coffee cup and said, "Lily, I don't want to live any days without you. I think we should get married."

I watched as her hand stilled and her eyes drifted upwards slowly, unreadable as she paused.

"Are you asking me? Or telling me?"

"I am asking you, sorry, if you want to. I understand if not, we never spoke about it, it is just—" She raised one finger up and rested it softly against my blabbering lips with a shush.

"So, ask me," she said softly.

"Lily," I pause and take a little breath, "Will you marry me?" I barely heard her excited yes as her lips crashed against mine.

And now here we are, just a few months away from our big day. It is entirely true what I said to Josh. Our small wedding has evolved and grown, but truth be told I don't actually mind. Lily isn't really a girly kind of girl and she is such a free-spirit so I hadn't expected her to embrace the idea of holy matrimony with such vigour. She devours magazines, watches trashy tv shows,

Pinterests and YouTubes anything and everything that had a wedding hashtag, and my office had slowly but surely been overtaken with all things bridal.

What I didn't say to Josh is it makes me feel like the luckiest woman in the world. That here is this stunning and brilliant girl and she spends hours and hours perfecting the day we will say our vows and promise ourselves to each other forever.

"What are you thinking about?" Lily asks me as we step into the elevator, the doors close with a ding and I turn to her. "I am thinking about how lucky I am and how I can't wait to get married."

"No, you weren't," she laughs, nudging me with her shoulder shyly.

"I absolutely was," I reply, my face serious because that touch is all it takes for that need to begin building up within me. I turn on the ball of my foot as my hands drop to the backs of her thighs and my knees bend a little. I slide my palms upwards and under her dress, gliding along her skin where I take handfuls of her sexy ass and lift her.

She gasps and leans back, her shoulders dragging up the mirror as I perch her on the rail that runs the length of the back of the elevator. I reach over to the pad and pull out the red emergency stop button and the lift slows to a halt.

"Frankie..." Lily says with a surprised voice but with a husky edge. I know she likes it when I take control, when I show her how much I want her—no, how much I need her. She perches on the bar, her body tilted so she can balance as I trail my nails up her shins. My thumbs press on her inner knees and with barely any pressure I spread her wider and slowly drop down.

My lips start at my thumbs and the soft, fleshy skin of her inner thigh and I work my way inwards. My nose trails along and I pause every few inches to suck her skin, to graze my teeth and bite her sweet flesh.

The smell of her drives me forwards, and her fingers reach down to pull up the hem of her dress until it rests bunched at her waist. Then her hands curl tight around the bar holding herself steady as I continue on my path. As I reach her panties it makes me wetter that they are white with blue spots and made of cotton.

That she can be so sexy and not even need to try.

My hands start their upwards path, and my thumbs hook under her panties and push them up. I gasp as I see the beautiful outline of her sex, those sweet puffy lips sandwiching her pink silky folds. I dive my head in and run my teeth downwards over the cotton, letting them scrape over her sensitive sex but softened slightly by the fabric.

Her moan edges me on, feeling her tremble my thumbs tighten and pull at the cotton, hooking with a force until I hear that soft tear at the seams. The soft golden hair between her legs is revealed in a ripped haze, the pads of my thumbs reach inwards and run over her creamy skin before I press upwards to display her.

I take a deep breath and watch how her pussy blossoms for me, licking my lips with a desperate hunger before I let out a long blow. I watch her tense, flex, the sensation causing her to tighten, and then I lean in. I start low and sweep my tongue inwards and upwards straight between her lips to take a full head-spinning taste of her.

I glance to the side and watch her hands tighten around the bar and the tiny thrust of her hips forward. I pull back a second to see her wetness glisten, letting her fill my senses before I dive back in again. This time I linger lower, my tongue lightly circling her entrance, widening her gently, slowly until my tongue slides in and she floods my mouth with her lust.

I feel my own wetness spreading. My own desire building as I make her writhe for me. My tongue moves up, sweeping through wet velvet, and I find her throbbing clit. My tongue lingers in a slow teasing circle, then flicks lightly. She lets out a slow, deep cry that echoes around the elevator and then I press my tongue flat against her, feeling the pulse of her as she vibrates.

I am obsessed now with chasing her orgasm, every time she bucks, I suck, when she writhes, I press. My lips closing around her so I can take soft, loving sucks of her gorgeous pussy before the fingers of my right hand push upwards and slowly enter her. She moans loudly. Her wetness is smeared across my lips, my chin, my cheeks. Covering me in her.

I feel the tension in her thighs. One hand leaves the rail and she grabs a handful of my hair. My fingers are fucking her deeply now and my mouth is on her clit. I feel her nails dig into my scalp and then she grips so hard my hair pulls at the follicles.

"Fuck... Frankie. Fuck, Fuck, Fuck...." She peppers each word with a moan, a cry, it runs through her entire body until she lets go and gives in to her orgasm.

I tilt my chin upwards so I can still feel the flood of her warmth across my face but can watch her as she rides each long wave. Her skin is flushed and glistening with sweat, trembling, shaking. The mirror behind her is steamy with her heat and I feel the change as her orgasm starts to subside and my mouth on her clit hits her wall of sensitivity. I could continue and make her orgasm again and again, but I can do that later. My fingers slide gently out of her.

I stand slowly, picking her panties up from the floor as I do and then gently take her in my arms, lowering her from the rail.

As I lean in, I feel her tongue sweep across my lips, tasting herself on me before giving me a hard, deep kiss.

"You are amazing," she murmurs against my lips and I pull her close and tight to me.

"No, you are." And I lean back and push in the red button, the lift whirs and clicks then shudders into action. She gives me the biggest, sexiest smile and within seconds the door pings open and we step out onto our floor as if nothing happened, but I see the glistening trail of cum down her bare leg and I want her all over again.

~

3 Months Later

Everything has been building to this moment as I stand at the top of the alter. My dad has already walked me down the aisle and is sitting beside my mum on the front row, both of their eyes shimmering with tears.

We haven't split the hall into sides, Lily

doesn't have family and most of our friends are just that—ours—so it is evenly filled and decorated to perfection. Lily has spent hours threading flowers, ribbons, love notes and small gifts for guests through trails along the seats.

I am wearing white, a dress, but very simple and sleek, long and fitted with long sleeves made from a fine lace. I am not a dress kind of girl, but I am a woman and I want to feel like a bride on my wedding day. My dark hair is pinned up with loose curls around my face and I even applied basic makeup—which YouTube helped me with. I look surprisingly good, I feel excited and I feel filled with love.

The music begins and I look straight to the back. She has chosen to walk alone, we talked a lot about it, my dad offered, but Lily decided that she wanted to leave the space for her brother, who she knew would be by her side today, if he could be.

And maybe he is.

As she steps out it is impossible for her to take my breath away as it is held so tight already in my lungs. Her lovely hair has been tamed into luscious curls framing her beautiful face, there are beautiful coloured flowers threaded through her hair and I can see the brightness of her eyes all the way from here. Her dress is not long, it is knee-length and loose and floaty, and her pale legs are on show in typical Lily style. It is stitched with beautiful flowers, sequins and thread that glitters and shimmers in the light. She is a vision and she will soon be my wife.

My gaze trails lower and I let out a small laugh which she catches and beams at because of her feet. Instead of pretty delicate sandals, high heels or sparkly shoes, she has chosen to wear her favourite black heeled ankle boots that glisten with a silver star on each side.

She looks like perfection.

It seems to take forever for her to reach me, but maybe it took no time at all. The second I am able to, I reach for her hand, needing to touch her, to be close to her as I drink in every inch of her beauty, trying to commit it all to memory so I will never forget this day or this moment.

We turn together, fingers entwined to

face the front as the music softens and the official begins to speak.

"We are gathered here today to join Frankie and Lily in marriage..."

I squeeze her soft fingers at the same moment as she squeezes mine, and I know I have found my happily ever after.

THE END

ALSO BY MARGAUX FOX

Thank you so much for reading this book. I really hope you enjoyed immersing yourself in Lily's World with Frankie. I have always been fascinated with the police and with criminals.

I perhaps watch too many crime shows on TV, but I love to write about forbidden love and the secrets that often come alongside them.

I would love for you to check out my other books if you haven't already and find me on social media @lovefrommargaux or on my website www.lovefrommargaux.com

FREE BOOK- You can pick up my story "Play With Me" for free if you sign up to my mailing list. I will update my mailing list with new releases, special offers and insights into my life and books.

Play
WITH ME
A LESBIAN SPORTS ROMANCE FROM
BEST-SELLING AUTHOR
MARGAUX FOX

FINDING
Haley
A LESBIAN ROMANCE
MARGAUX FOX

What happens when a mysterious and dangerously attractive stranger comes crashing into a detective's life?

getbook.at/FFH

Neither woman can stop thinking about their perfect first love with each other from so many years ago. Can they find a way to get it back?

getbook.at/HCC

Printed in Great Britain
by Amazon

58661408R00108